BEFORE THE KILLING (Book One)

"Once I started I couldn't put it down!"
-Bookshelf Adventures

"Mystery fans will love this plot device, which takes a straightforward whodunit to an otherworldly level."
-The BookLife Prize

"A cleverly plotted fantasy thriller with a strong cast of characters."
-The Wishing Shelf Book Awards

BEFORE SHE WAS TAKEN (Book Two)

"This was such an amazing novel to read... The characters were wonderfully written and very easy to like. I found myself unable to put it down... This novel was a fast read for me and I greatly recommend it. I can't wait to continue with the series in the future." -Bookshelf Adventures

"The plot moves at an even pace and has a surprising ending; this supernatural mystery will be enjoyed by a diverse array of readers... the book has a strong female character who is easy to follow, smart, and displays agency."
-The BookLife Prize

BEFORE THE KILLING

The Killing Hour Book One

MARGIE BENEDICT

FIRST EDITION, JANUARY 2021

This is a work of fiction. Names, characters, businesses, places, events, and
incidents are either the products of the author's imagination or used in a
fictitious manner. Any resemblance to actual persons, living or dead, or
actual events is purely coincidental.

Publisher: margiebenedict.com
Cover Design: GetCovers.com

ISBN: 978-1-954584-23-5 (paperback)

Printed in the United States of America

For First Love

Prologue

CASSIE (AGE 26)

CASSIE, who lives alone, has just turned out the light in the kitchen when an unusual sight draws her gaze to the window. Countless lights fill the night sky, like bright pinpricks in a cloak of black velvet. Fascinated, she goes outside to gaze at them. The display overwhelms her with a wondrous feeling regarding the vastness of the universe. She actually finds it soothing to be reminded of the relative insignificance of her life and the mostly disastrous trajectory it's followed so far.

The lights grow brighter, or maybe just closer. One in particular increases in intensity until it seems to be heading straight for her house. Fearful, she backs inside planning to slam the door shut, but then the thing arcs downward and disappears behind the hedges. The leaves rustle.

Her cat Gio rubs against her leg. His fur is sticking straight up on his back, and his eyes bulge like yellow marbles, staring at the place where something might've landed. Cassie has goosebumps herself, but still can't resist going to check. Peering behind the bushes, she sees a small rock glowing like a piece of lit charcoal. When she moves aside branches to get a closer look, a spark flies out and pricks her bare arm. It doesn't burn but causes a tingling sensation.

The glow of the meteorite or whatever-it-is has already dimmed by the time she shifts her gaze back to it. Now it just looks like the kind of granite found everywhere in this area. Since it's sitting in the dirt not touching anything, she doesn't think it's in any danger of starting a fire even if it's still hot. She decides to leave it for now. She can collect it tomorrow when it's definitely cooled down, and possibly take it somewhere like the Museum of Science in Boston. Or maybe call them first to be sure they would be interested. It could be that meteorites land all the time and scientists already have warehouses full of them.

Under the glare of the outdoor lamp, she examines her arm. The spark left a small red mark, but it doesn't hurt when she touches it. However, a sudden sense of unease makes her quicken her steps back into the house. Gio slips between her feet before she shuts the door firmly behind them and snaps the bolt.

Part One: Witness

CASSIE (AGE 19)

Chapter One

THE MURDER HAPPENED on June 9th or 10th, 1973, the day (or two) after Cassie came home for the summer following her first year at Syracuse. Apparently, the last breath was drawn so close to midnight, the medical examiner couldn't say with certainty whether it came before or after, though officially the death was certified as occurring on Sunday, the 10th.

Cassie woke early on the 9th, not that she had any premonition regarding what was to come, but because she couldn't wait to see Julian after so much time apart. At five a.m., diffused sunshine already filled her room, and birds were singing in a chorus outside her window.

Rising and crossing to the study that looked out toward the back of her house, she gazed at the sights she'd missed since Christmas. The still gray surface of Inner Harbor… the large grassy backyard sloping down to a border of mud where the water lapped up… the encircling branches of the gnarled oak she used to climb with her friends. From the side window, she glimpsed crows lined up on the roof of their red barn. Beyond that, past the edge of their property, the familiar gravestones poked up in a scattered formation across the hillside cemetery. She would soon pay one of them a visit.

A feeling rose inside her that was half-adrenaline, half-aching heart for this place that formed an essential part of her. She didn't know if she'd have the strength to leave it again come fall, but that was something she preferred not to think about just yet. She settled back into her father's old chair and stared out at the wakening world for an hour at least. She may have dozed off.

Eventually she returned to her bedroom to be confronted by the two suitcases and five cardboard boxes she'd carried up from the car last night. She would've rather ignored them and gone directly to Julian's, but when she spoke on the phone with him before she left Syracuse, he said he would be out with his father on the boat this morning.

Therefore, she dove into the unpacking and rather quickly had her clothes put away in her closet and dresser. But when she reached the box that held her Julian mementos, it slowed her down. She sat on the bed and flipped open the photo album, going through each picture like a preview of coming attractions. Julian and her in his father's truck, on the lobsterboat, at the beach, canoeing across Inner Harbor, on the rollercoaster at Escapade Park.

After the photos, came the contents of her special carved wooden box. The earrings he gave her for her eighteenth birthday. The roses—now dried—he bought for graduation. The letters—too few—he sent her during their separation. She raised her right hand to gaze for the millionth time at the silver ring he gave her before she left in September. It was a simple, plain band but what mattered was his pledge to be true to her forever.

Before closing up the boxes again, she removed the cassette recording of a piano recital Julian had done in high school. Debussy's *Rêverie*, one of the most exquisite songs she'd ever heard, and Julian played it masterfully. Not that she was any kind of expert, but his performance managed to silence an auditorium full of rowdy teenagers, which was saying quite a lot. She had listened to the tape often while she was away.

When nearly everything was back in its place, the phone rang, making her leap in response. She dashed down the hall and through the open door into her mother's bedroom, glad to see her mother had already risen and gone somewhere else in the house. "I'll get it!" Cassie shouted, lifting the receiver.

"Hello?" She made her voice soft and sultry, thinking it would be Julian on the other end.

Her heart sank when it wasn't. "Oh hi, Mr. Harrington." *Ew.* She felt weird having used her sexy voice on her mother's boyfriend. He was saying something to her now, but she pretended not to hear, cupping the receiver and calling out to her mother. She hung up the second the phone was picked up in the kitchen.

Cassie returned to her room to change out of her pajamas. Anticipating a hot day, she put on her bikini and topped it with a tank top and cutoffs. She braided her hair in the back, and dabbed on lipstick and eyeliner before heading downstairs to get breakfast.

Her mother was still on the phone. Cassie tried to ignore the conversation while preparing a bowl of granola with milk and sliced banana. She glanced through the newspaper headlines while she ate, though mostly she was focused on thoughts of her upcoming day.

Eventually her mother hung up and announced she was going to a party with Mr. Harrington tonight. She came up behind Cassie and played with her braid.

"That's nice," Cassie said. Since she expected to be with

Julian, she wasn't sure why her mother bothered to tell her. She knew one of Mr. Harrington's daughters, making it awkward the father of this girl she hung out with a few times was now dating her mother. However, he was divorced, and Cassie's mother was a widow, and there probably weren't a lot of eligible people their age in this small town.

"Let's plan dinner together for Sunday." Her mother patted her shoulder absentmindedly. "I missed you while you were away."

"Mm, me too." She got up to rinse off her dishes. "I'm going to Julian's."

"Of course you are." Her mother smiled. "Take the car if you like."

Cassie glanced out the window at clear blue sky. "I'll ride my bike." Brumewich, Massachusetts, where she lived, was compact enough that most anywhere she might want to go lay within a thirty-minute bike ride. This, despite that homes were stretched out from one another, separated by luxurious lawns and hundreds-of-years-old trees. They were spoiled by an excess of natural beauty, here in Brumewich.

"Be careful, honey," her mother said. "Last week a car hit a bicyclist on Sand Road in Ruford. The boy broke his nose."

"Yeah, don't worry, Mom," she said, though she knew it was wasted advice. For every possible way that one might get injured or die, her mother could dig up a recent example from the news.

Fifteen minutes after setting out, Cassie approached Julian's rather rundown house, located across the street from the main commercial dock. Since it was a Saturday in June, the harbor was bustling, between the fishing boats coming back in for the day, and the pleasure boats heading out. Passing near the water, she looked out to see if Julian had arrived. She spotted the Reis boat, but only Armando, his father, was there tidying up a few things. He didn't notice her, and she didn't call out to him, figuring there would be plenty of time to greet him later.

Armando's Chevy pickup was parked in the driveway, outside their carport. She had painted an orange lobster on the back of its cargo bed last summer, and it pleased her to see the colors hadn't faded. She laid her bike down on the lawn that was more dirt and weeds than grass. The uneasy sense of someone's eyes on her made her glance back before approaching the house. A young woman, Teresa Patterson, leaned against the side of a rusty green Volkswagen Bug across the street.

Cassie remembered her from high school, though Teresa was older, a senior when she was a freshman. It really wasn't possible to forget the older girl, because of how gorgeous she was. Whenever she passed by in the corridor, every boy's eyes would be on her. Behind her back, they called her Raquel—because of the actress Raquel Welch. Seriously, she was that sexy. But despite all of them lusting after her, Cassie couldn't recall her dating anyone in particular.

Teresa looked as amazing as ever, in a little white dress that exposed cleavage on top, and long, tanned legs beneath. When she noticed Cassie looking, she shifted her gaze to the dock and waved at someone down below.

Cassie turned back to the house. Julian was likely inside taking a shower, as he always did immediately after getting off the boat, wanting to scrub off the fishy odor. Funny thing, she actually loved that smell. She was a child of the sea and always would be.

The Reis family, father and son, never locked their doors, night or day, home or not home. She assumed they kept their money in the bank, and what else would anyone want to steal? The thrift store furniture? The record player from

1943? The rickety upright piano that Julian—defying all odds and sour notes—had learned to play like a god?

An unlocked home was not unusual in Brumewich, though. Whenever a visitor encountered one, they were expected to knock first to announce their presence, then go right in before anyone inside might be forced to rise from their chair to get the door.

Cassie followed protocol, but it threw her off to find Julian frozen in the center of the family room, looking at her like she'd caught him in the middle of an embarrassing act. His hand that was balled up in a fist moved into his pocket where he may have deposited something.

Though he clearly wanted to hide the object, she would still have asked him about it if he hadn't distracted her immediately. He broke into a smile that lit up his face, sweeping away her brief suspicion. "Cass!" He crossed the room in two steps, lifted her in his arms, and swung her around in a full circle. "Cass, I missed you."

She raised her hands to his neck and kissed him, breathing in the familiar scent of warm citrus that came from his shampoo, and releasing the longing she'd felt through the snowbound winter and the drenching spring in Syracuse. Eventually they drew back just to look at each other. His expression shone with good humor, over-confidence, and carelessness in equal amounts. It made her jealous to see how brown he was already, though summer had barely begun. He'd inherited rapid-tanning skin along with glossy black hair from his Portuguese dad.

"Where were you last night?" She'd been hoping he might come to her house and surprise her.

"Me? I was home."

"I called. No one answered."

"What time?"

"I don't know. Past ten."

"Oh yeah? I was asleep."

"That's pathetic," she said.

"My father gets me up at four-thirty."

"Oh all right." She kissed him again. "Did you miss me very much?"

"Are you crazy? I couldn't think of anything else."

"Good. I hope you suffered a lot while I was gone."

"I'll suffer even more if I don't get something to eat." He went into the kitchen with Cassie following directly behind.

"You're not hungry, are you?" Julian foraged for sandwich ingredients in the fridge and cupboards. He was always famished after he came back from the boat.

"I'll take everything you have," she said to spite him. The front door opened and a moment later, Armando entered the kitchen.

"Look who's back from college." He gave her a warm smile. "You're gonna get a big hug but not before I clean up."

"Nice to see you, Armando." Mr. Reis always insisted Cassie use his first name.

"He tell you what happened?" Armando nodded in Julian's direction.

"He never tells me anything," she said.

"Papai, forget it." Julian looked annoyed.

But Armando launched into his story. "This mornin' on the boat, he's got a trap balanced on the side. I tell him to heave it. He shoves it off and stands there in a daze while rope flies out of the hot water barrel, you know, followin' the trap down." He paused for effect. "So my fool kid gets his leg in the way. Know how fast that thing goes, Cassie?"

She nodded her head, because she did know. She'd been on the boat once when Julian was setting traps.

"The line's tightening round his leg, pullin' him down,

draggin' him to the edge… he's strugglin' to free himself but he can't. So who do you think saves him? I grab my knife, saw at the rope… friggin' hard to cut it. Meanwhile my son's holdin' onto the side for dear life."

"Obviously you managed it since I'm standing right here," Julian said.

"You bet I did. But thanks to you, we lost a perfectly good trap."

"How's your leg, Julian?" she said.

"Fine. My father's exaggerating."

"Gonna have a good bruise there in the morning," Armando said. "And you're welcome."

"Thanks, Papai." Julian gave him a sheepish look. Sometimes, the way they spoke to each other reminded her of brothers rather than father and son. Partly because his dad was only eighteen when Julian was born. And mostly because his mom died in childbirth and it had been just the two of them since then. Cassie had never seen a parent and child that were closer.

"Why weren't you paying attention?" she asked Julian.

"Couldn't wait to see his girl." Armando looked at Julian's developing sandwich. "You gonna share that with her?"

"Cass, you want some?" Without waiting for her reply, he added, "She's not hungry."

Just for that, she swiped a piece of cheese from on top of his bread and stuck it in her mouth.

"I taught you better manners than that," Armando told him. His gaze shifted to the table. "And after she was so nice and brought you a cookie."

She followed his eyes to a sugar cookie shaped like a heart, resting on a napkin on the table. "Oh I didn't bring that." She looked at Julian. "Where'd you get it?"

When Julian didn't answer, Armando said, "Must be from my secret admirer." He took the cookie and walked away.

"He has a secret admirer?" she whispered after he'd gone out.

Julian snorted. "Pete dropped it by earlier." She did think it was odd, though, that he hadn't said that right away.

They set out in the truck after he demolished his sandwich in several huge bites.

"Beach?" she asked him as he backed out of the driveway.

He gave her a sideways glance with half-lidded eyes that told her he had something else in mind.

"Surprise me," she said.

Before long, he drove to the end of an empty road, where a residential construction site lay deserted. "I don't think anyone works here on Saturdays." He parked the Chevy under the shade of an elm tree on the side.

It wasn't their first time doing it in the truck, and they knew how to manage the limited space. Amazing what one can accomplish when the desire is strong enough. He grabbed a condom from the glove compartment, and it did worry her a little to see what a ready supply he had despite her being out of town for months. But it could've been Armando's stash. Last summer, he'd been dating a woman ten years his junior.

The cramped quarters and months spent apart rendered their love-making frenzied and ecstatic. But the best part to Cassie was when he gathered her in his arms afterward and she listened to the rhythm of his heart. Here was home in the best possible sense.

Their repose didn't last long. At the sound of an approaching vehicle, they sprung apart and scrambled to locate discarded clothing. As soon as Julian had on his shorts, he started up the truck and headed back the way they'd come. Cassie was pulling on her T-shirt as they passed the middle-aged couple—probably the property owners—who looked amused.

When they reached the road, they exchanged a glance and burst out laughing. "Beach now?" Julian said.

"Hell yeah."

He drove them to Thorne Cove, which they liked better than Gull Beach, crowded with families this time of year. The cove had a cottage beyond the sand line, and was, strictly speaking, a private section of the coast shared among a dozen or so homeowners. But this early in the season most of the summer dwellers had not yet arrived, meaning no one was around to complain about their trespassing. The beach itself was small, with trees on one side and rocks jutting out into the water on the other.

She and Julian played like they were eight years old. They swam in the bitter-cold ocean, and when they needed to get warm, they sat near the water's edge and built a castle. Then back in to rinse off, and onto the beach where Julian buried her under the sand and threatened to leave her there.

Later while Cassie lay in the deliciously warming sun, Julian practiced diving off the rocks. She turned her head sideways to watch him. It filled her with awe that this tall man with a Grecian nose, sculpted torso, and powerful arms that must've come from all the work hauling traps... that this extraordinarily handsome man had pledged himself to her.

Three teenage girls had recently arrived and set their towels close to where he was diving. They sat there watching him while they spread baby oil all over their bodies. From the way they giggled and whispered among themselves, Cassie knew they were talking about him, maybe even daring each other to go speak to him.

When he got out of the water, he actually swaggered past the girls on his way to Cassie, showing how much he enjoyed the attention. So naturally she kicked sand on him as soon as he was close. In response he leapt on her and kissed her with the taste of salt water on his tongue.

During the drive back to his house, she asked him what they should do tonight.

"Sorry, I'm gonna be busy," he said.

"What do you mean?"

"Me and my friends are hanging out at Escapade Park."

"Can't I come?"

"It's only guys tonight. One of them just got dumped by his girlfriend."

"Which friends are these?"

"They're from Ruford. You don't know them."

"I thought you would've saved tonight for me," she said.

"Tomorrow is yours." He reached over and squeezed her hand. "Day and night. And the day and night after that. And so on for the rest of our lives, except when I need to work."

She wasn't happy, spending her first full night home without Julian. Jealousy niggled at her, and she couldn't help being afraid his plans might have something to do with Teresa Patterson, aka Raquel. She even wondered if thoughts of how he was going to choose between them might've been what distracted him on the boat this morning. But she told herself that was ridiculous.

Chapter Two

AFTER RETURNING from her afternoon with Julian, she made a grilled cheese sandwich for dinner. Her mother came down while Cassie was eating. She'd really outdone herself with her makeup, a satiny silver sleeveless dress, and killer high heels.

"What'd you do with my mother?" Cassie teased. Possibly for the first time ever, she noticed the way her sky-blue eyes contrasted prettily with the rich nutty color of her hair, and how slender she still looked despite her age.

"It's still me in here," her mother said. "Are you going back to Julian's?"

She shook her head. "He's busy."

Her mother was barely listening. "Then could you bring this to Mrs. Wolcott after you finish eating?" She pointed at a large box resting on the floor. "Clothing donations. She's taking them to that non-profit where she's on the board."

"Does it have to be tonight?"

"She said she wanted to deliver everything early tomorrow." The doorbell rang. "Mr. Harrington's here." She patted down her hair and smoothed her skirt before opening the front door. "Hi Freddie."

Mr. Harrington—*Freddie*—peered into the house and across the hall at Cassie sitting at the kitchen table. "Cassie, you're home!"

She wasn't sure how to respond to such an obvious statement. "Yup, here I am."

"Ellen's back too." This was his daughter who was Cassie's age. "I know she'd love to see you."

She seriously doubted that. Ellen and her siblings had gone to private school. They had a whole different set of friends. "Sure, sounds good," she said.

"Thanks for helping me out," her mother said. "The party may go late. Don't wait up for us." She laughed at her little joke of pretending their roles were reversed, as she stepped past Mr. Harrington, heading to his Mercedes Benz parked in the driveway.

Cassie wasn't sure what her mother saw in him. She'd witnessed him bowing and scraping to Mrs. Wolcott at a Memorial Day gathering one time, and he also looked down his nose at the people who worked behind the counter at the lobster pound. Immigrants like Armando Reis, for example. If Mr. Harrington were some sort of Adonis maybe she could understand her mother's willingness to overlook his character flaws. Unfortunately, he was the opposite. Bald on top of his head, he let the thin strands of hair on the back and sides grow down to his shoulders. No doubt he believed the long hair made him cool, but actually he just looked like Benjamin Franklin. She figured her mother wanted financial stability and tried not to judge her. Cassie's father had been her soulmate, and a person couldn't expect to find more than one of those in a lifetime.

After washing her dinner dishes, Cassie hoisted the box

and carried it out to the car. She approached the Wolcott place following a short drive, and couldn't help pausing to gape since she hadn't seen it in some time. The centerpiece of the estate was an enormous white Colonial house. But like a vacation resort, it also included a private dock, tennis court, putting green, swimming pool, and a matching (but considerably smaller) white Colonial guesthouse. All this spread across several acres of carpetlike lawn amid clusters of trees pruned to match each other.

Grant's mother and father, who had dementia now, occupied the entire mansion themselves. Maybe staff lived there too, she wasn't sure. Needless to say, they were the richest family in town, and probably among the top five in Massachusetts. She couldn't imagine Mrs. Wolcott needing Mom's bargain-basement hand-me-downs. The woman probably was donating silks and fur coats. But Cassie's mother had been sucking up to her lately, possibly due to Mr. Harrington's influence. He was a social climber if ever there was one.

She rounded the circular drive that led to the front door; it was like a grand hotel entrance. After parking, she ascended the marble steps flanked by pillars to ring the bell at their massive, double-sided front door. She expected a butler to answer and inform her in a British accent, "Deliveries are in the back."

But instead, Mrs. Wolcott's son Grant opened the door. It surprised Cassie to see him, though she should've expected he'd be home from school now too. He was a few years older than her; probably in his senior year. It struck her his appearance had changed significantly for the better. His hair, neatly combed and cut rather short compared to other guys his age, had a golden sheen to it. His light blue eyes were arresting, though his face might've been bland if not for the hawk nose that added character and interest. He was also taller than she remembered and had shed all of his youthful pudge.

At the moment he appeared to be annoyed about something, which she assumed was her, showing up unannounced on his doorstep. But a second later, his features formed into a pleasant mask. "Cassie?"

"Yeah, hi Grant. How are you?"

"Not bad. You're back for the summer?"

"Right, got home from Syracuse yesterday." No point in explaining she might not return there in the fall. "You too?"

"Graduated a month ago," he said. "I'm working in Boston this summer."

"Really? Doing what?"

"Interning at HarborBanks. It's kind of boring."

"I hope it gets better." She glanced around. "Are you living here?" She tried not to sound like she was making fun of him for still being with his parents.

"In the guesthouse. Going to Wharton in the fall. You know, business school."

"Cool." *And that's how the rich get richer.* She turned back and pointed at the open trunk. "I brought a clothing donation from my mom. Can you ask someone to carry it in?" Frankly, she didn't see why she should do it, when they probably had a houseful of servants being paid for work like this.

But Grant came down the steps to lift out the box himself.

"Hey, I didn't mean you," she said.

"I don't mind. Thanks for bringing it."

It suddenly occurred to her to wonder if her mother included some of her old things in the donation. She should've checked. It mortified her imagining Grant seeing her crappy old clothing and laughing at it, or worse, feeling sorry for her.

He paused holding the box and looked at her. "Are you

still seeing Julian Reis?" It was odd, but she got the impression he was trying to cover the seriousness of the question with a casual tone.

"Yeah, why?"

"Um, I just thought you would've broken up. When you went to college."

"Nope. Not at all. We're good." Her voice sounded more defensive than she felt.

"Are you sure he… never mind, it's not my business."

"What do you mean?" she said.

"Nothing. I think it's great you're still together." He stepped toward the house. "Thanks for the donation." He carried the box inside and closed the door.

She wasn't sure what to make of their conversation. Did he know something about Julian she wasn't aware of? Or was he fishing to ask her out himself? She cursed him under her breath, annoyed he re-awakened the suspicions she'd been trying to suppress all day.

When she got back home it was still light out. She gathered a mixed bouquet of flowers from the garden to bring to her father, whose gravesite she hadn't visited since Christmas. The entrance to the cemetery adjoined their property and may have been what kept the price of their harborside home low enough for her parents to afford it. For a reason Cassie didn't understand, some people drew the line at having dead folks as neighbors.

The cemetery with its grassy knolls and twisted oaks was dear to her. Some of its graves were from two and a half centuries ago. There were sculptures of swans and sleeping children, and monuments to drowned sailors and soldiers that fell in battle. Their beloved Brumewich ancestors, all.

Her father's grave was on a hill overlooking Inner Harbor. She laid the flowers at his headstone and sat to watch the colors of the sunset reflected in the water while her thoughts wandered back to her memories of him. A moment of calm in an otherwise confusing day.

It was nearly dark by the time she rose again. A noise came from somewhere at the bottom of the hill. When she looked down the path, she thought she saw a shadow disappear behind a tree. Probably her imagination; hardly anyone came to the cemetery at night. Nevertheless, she quickened her pace to the gate, and from there to her house.

Afterward she went to her room and did some sketching because it was too early to go to bed. When she heard the car drive up outside, she shut off her light and peeked out her window at the front. Mr. Harrington walked her mother to the door and looked like he wanted to follow her inside. She shook her head, probably recoiling from the idea of Cassie being home and them doing it in the bedroom next to hers. At least Cassie was recoiling from that idea.

He got a little aggressive with her, but she pushed him firmly away and he finally turned back to his car. His steps wove on his way there, and he looked too drunk to get behind the wheel of any vehicle, but she just went in the house and shut the door behind her. Cassie was surprised her mother would ignore his condition, considering what happened to her father. She tried not to think about it, looking away, not wanting to see just how bad his driving might be. Not wanting to be reminded of her father's accident.

Floorboards creaked as her mother made her way upstairs. Cassie expected she would glance in and was surprised to hear her footsteps continue past the door into her own room. Within a few more minutes all was silent. Her mother might've been too plastered to remember her daughter was back from school. Most likely she fell face down on the bed and passed out immediately without even taking off her high heels.

Unlike her, Cassie was wide awake. The time was only 10:40, which made her laugh after her mother saying they were going to be out late. Apparently that was late to them.

Putting away her sketchpad, she thought of Julian, wondering if he might have gotten home from his night out with his friends. If so, it would be lovely to sneak into his house and up the stairs to his bedroom. She could think of no reason why they shouldn't sleep together tonight. And if he wasn't home yet, she could wait and surprise him when he arrived. Armando in his bedroom downstairs would never notice a thing.

She put on a light summer dress and gave her hair a quick brush. Pausing outside her mother's room, she was glad to hear her heavy breathing. Down the stairs and out the side door she went. Her first thought was to take the car, but she decided to go by bike rather than take the chance the engine would wake her mother and possibly make her worry about where Cassie had gone.

Besides, she loved riding at night when the streets were empty. She flicked on the bike light and set out along the route that skirted the shore, which was less likely to have traffic at this time. To her great surprise, however, she spotted Julian's truck parked along the side of the road just before the turnoff to Thorne Cove. She couldn't miss it with her very own lobster painted on the back.

At first she thought he and his friends must've gone to the beach with a six-pack or a nickel of grass after getting back from the amusement park. She even turned down the lane, thinking it might be fun to surprise him, though a second later she stopped. If she showed up there, it could embarrass him. His friends might mock him over his girlfriend following him wherever he went.

While she was hesitating, she noticed the rusted green VW Bug parked farther up the lane. The car Teresa had been leaning on in the morning. It had to be hers.

She breathed hard. Could it be? Had Julian lied to her? Had he been cheating with Teresa all year long?

Her initial thought was to march right onto the beach and confront them. But she realized she couldn't do it. Even imagining Teresa in his arms was too much for her. If she were to see them together with her own eyes, she might as well just tear out her own heart and stomp all over it.

She rode hard back toward home, except for pausing three times to wipe away the tears that blinded her.

Chapter Three

"CASSIE?" Her mother's shout from what sounded like two feet away woke her up.

"What?!" She was disoriented, like the space between her ears was filled with cotton instead of a brain. Failing to block out thoughts of Julian sneaking around behind her back with Teresa, she'd suffered a long, miserable, sleepless night, until finally drifting off close to sunrise.

Her mother sat on the bed beside her and rubbed her arm. "There's terrible news. Do you remember Teresa Patterson?"

Cassie blinked at her mother, thinking: *Remember her? I don't expect to ever forget her for the rest of my life.*

Her mother didn't wait for an answer. "I think she's a few years older than you. I mean, was a few years older. She's been murdered. Someone found her body early this morning at Thorne Cove." She squeezed Cassie's arm. "Thank god you didn't go out last night."

"Murdered?" Cassie couldn't wrap her head around the

word. "Murdered?" she repeated, pulling herself up in the bed.

"That's what they're saying. The police haven't let out how, though. And they haven't caught anyone. If it's someone with a gun, the police ought to warn us. What if there's a shooter loose in town?"

"At Thorne Cove? Is that what you said?" Cassie's brain was struggling to keep up.

"Yes, honey. Thorne Cove. Are you all right? I know it's shocking news."

"What about Julian?" She had a horrific vision of their bullet-ridden, blood-soaked bodies side-by-side on the sand.

"Julian? What does he have to do with it?"

Her mother didn't know he'd been there with Teresa. Maybe no one knew. Except her. "Oh, I… I'm confused. I was just having a dream about him." Teresa must've died later, after Julian left. "What time was she killed?"

"How should I know? That's for the police examiner to figure out. Sometime during the night."

"Are you sure it was her?"

"Of course. Franny Thatcher lives right across from there and she's been out talking to the police."

"But are they sure it's murder? Maybe it was an accident. Or suicide."

"I don't think so. Franny sounded sure."

Her head was throbbing. Julian had been there. But it couldn't have anything to do with him. Whatever happened must have taken place after he went home. There couldn't be any doubt about that.

"Maybe it was a serial killer," her mother said. "He could've been stalking her. She was very pretty, wasn't she? That's what Franny told me."

"A serial killer? In Brumewich?" It was just like her mother to hit on a theory like that.

"Why not? Boston had the Boston Strangler. Someone like that could be anywhere. We'll have to lock all our doors and windows from now on."

"Whoever it is, they better catch him soon." Cassie lowered the sheet to get up.

"Did I ever meet Teresa? Was she a friend of yours?" her mother said.

"She was older. We weren't friends. What senior hangs out with a freshman?" She reached for her clothes.

"Where are you going?" Her mother's voice held an edge of panic.

"Julian's." It was the first thing that crossed Cassie's mind. She would go to his house and confirm for herself he had nothing to do with this.

"No. There's a killer out there. It might be some crazy person with a gun." Her mother was back on the shooter theory.

"I doubt it's anything like that. I bet whoever did this is long gone. I'll be careful though. I'm sure if there's any danger, the cops will set up a roadblock. Let me take the car." At least that would keep her mother from worrying about bike accidents.

Before they could continue their argument, the phone rang. Cassie's mother jumped up, unable to resist answering it. "Fine, but don't stay out long," she told her daughter as she hurried to her own room to pick up the call. Another one of her friends, no doubt. This would likely continue all day.

Cassie felt numb as she got dressed. She grabbed an apple on the way out the door and ate it in the car, taking the alternate route to Julian's, avoiding the turnoff to the cove. Likely that way would be blocked anyhow, to keep gawkers away while police continued to gather evidence at the cove. Town residents would be curious. An unexpected death was rare in Brumewich.

When she reached the Reis house, she found Armando outside, vacuuming the inside of the Chevy. It struck her odd that he would pick a time like this to clean it. She couldn't help wondering if it was related to the truck having been at Thorne Cove last night.

Noticing her approach, Armando shut off the vacuum. His eyes were red like he'd been weeping. "You heard the news?" he said.

She nodded.

"What kind a monster would do a thing like that?" He turned back to his truck. "Julian's inside," he said hoarsely.

He was taking it so hard, he made her fear Julian might somehow be involved. On the other hand, it made sense Armando would be anxious about the appearance of guilt that came from his son being at the wrong place at the wrong time. The Reis family was not of the privileged class. Armando had arrived in America with nothing, and since then he and his son had worked with their hands and sweat to make a passable living. Their kind of people never dared admit anything because they knew it would be used against them. They understood if anyone were going to take the fall for a crime, it was going to be them.

Entering the house, she called out to Julian. Right away he emerged from his dad's room, for some reason, and hugged her hard. His throat was thick when he spoke. "Hey. You must've heard. I can't believe it."

"I feel so bad for her." Tears stung her eyes. She longed to open up to him and tell him what she'd seen last night. She wanted to beg him for an explanation. She wanted him to swear he had nothing to do with it. But she kept quiet because—more than anything—she needed to hang onto her belief in his innocence for as long as possible.

"Is there any more news? You know, like, how she died?" he said.

She shook her head.

He echoed his father. "Who would do a thing like that?"

"A serial killer." That was her mother's theory and she was sticking to it. "When did you hear?"

"My father was up early like usual. He overheard somebody talking about it at the market."

"I guess you were out late with your friends." It was the closest she dared get to asking him what he was doing last night.

He hesitated. "Not that late. I, um…"

It seemed like he was about to speak openly. But with the worst timing possible, two police cars turned onto the harbor road and squealed to a halt right outside the house. She and Julian watched through the open door as four officers, one in plainclothes, got out of the vehicles and stalked up the driveway looking grim. Armando, now spraying the outside of the truck with hose water, looked like the proverbial cat caught with a mouthful of mouse. Julian's face paled.

The one who wasn't wearing a uniform approached Armando. "Detective Heath." He shook Armando's hand. "Mind if we talk to your son?"

"What for?" Sweat glistened from Armando's brow.

"We have some questions for him, related to Teresa Patterson's murder."

"Got nothin' to do with Julian."

"Probably not. But it will help us if we can clear up a couple things," the detective said.

"You got a warrant?" Armando said.

The detective raised an eyebrow. "Like I said, it's just a

few questions. We're trying not to escalate things. We'll get a warrant if you insist. If you're worried he's involved."

Cassie wondered if that was even legal, suggesting that insisting on getting a warrant made a person look guilty.

Julian came down the steps from the house. "Papai, it's okay, I'll talk to them."

She wanted to scream, *don't do it, make them get a warrant, give yourselves time to figure out a strategy. Don't let them rush you into this or you'll regret it.*

"Can we go inside?" Detective Heath said.

"Sure." Julian moved aside for him.

When Armando tried to follow, the detective stopped him. "Wait here, please, Mr. Reis." He glanced at the truck. "That's enough cleaning for now. I'll have my officers bring out a chair if you'd like to sit."

"Don't need a chair." Armando glared at them.

The detective finally glanced at Cassie. "You should go home, miss."

Her eyes went to Julian for confirmation. He nodded and said, "Call you later."

Trying her hardest to keep her expression unconcerned, she made her way past them to her car.

Chapter Four

CASSIE DROVE HOME TO WAIT. She really didn't know what else to do. Her mother had left a note on the kitchen counter saying she was at Mr. Harrington's house. *Good.* Cassie had not been looking forward to facing a barrage of questions from her.

Needing an activity to fill her time until she might hear from Julian again, she went to her studio in the barn. She set up her palette and easel to continue work on a painting she'd begun during winter break. It was the image of a woman with wind-whipped hair leaning over an as-yet-unnamed gravestone while dark clouds gathered overhead. The subject of death now seemed prescient.

Outside, the weather was starting to resemble what was depicted in her painting. A rare June nor'easter had been forecast for tonight, and already the wind hissed through the cracks in the barn, and light rain pattered on the roof.

Several hours must've passed before she heard his footsteps. Julian came rushing into the building, his hair and jacket damp, his expression wild. She lowered her paintbrush.

Part of her wanted to run to him, but the other part was filled with resentment and suspicion. She remained in place.

But Julian, not noticing her reticence, swept her into his arms anyway. He kissed her hair, her cheek, her lips, and even her hand. "I'm fucked."

She drew back. "Tell me everything." She meant it, too. She was ready for him to pour out every bit of the truth to her, however much it might hurt to hear it.

"The cops are getting a warrant to search our house."

"I'm sure there's nothing to find. Why you? Why your house?" *Explain to me why you were with her at Thorne Cove last night*, she wanted to say, but held back.

"I don't know. They're not telling us anything."

You're lying. You were with her and somehow they've figured that out. This was the point when her heart hardened against him. He was so determined to keep the truth from her, it made her question whether she'd ever really known him at all.

She kept up the façade of believing him. "It should be easy to prove you had nothing to do with it. You were out with your friends last night."

Guilt flashed in his eyes. "We didn't stay out very long. I left them around ten and went home. I wanted to see you, but I couldn't stay awake. Problem is, I'm screwed without an alibi for later in the night."

"What about your father? Wasn't he home?"

"He was sleeping. Didn't even hear me come in. You know how he is."

This much was likely true. His father never seemed to hear anything after he went to his room for the evening.

"Even if he wanted to lie and say he was awake and we were watching TV or some shit like that, it wouldn't matter. He'd say anything to protect me. Any parent would."

"I guess," she said, though she imagined there might be parents who wouldn't.

"So I'm asking… and it's totally okay if you say no… I'm asking if you'll be my alibi."

She had guessed this was coming and still it made her insides tighten. "You want me to lie for you?" Because that was exactly what he was asking. And she wouldn't have minded so very much if she didn't know there was something essential he was holding back. She would've happily lied for him if she didn't know for a fact he was at the cove last night.

He could've said something… could've explained why he'd needed to meet with Teresa… even if the explanation was that he'd fallen in love with her. At least then Cassie wouldn't think he was a liar as well as a cheater.

"I'm sorry. I wouldn't ask if I wasn't desperate. You know? But it's okay if you don't want to do it."

"Didn't the police already ask where you were last night? And who you were with? You can't change your story now, can you?"

This stopped Julian dead. She had called his bluff, apparently. The stuff about *it's okay if you don't want to do it* was coming too late.

"You're right… I already told them you were with me. I had to come up with something on the spot. Christ, they were making me sweat. But I really mean it, if you don't want to lie, you don't have to. I'll go back and tell them the truth. I'll just say what I said to you: I was afraid they'd never believe me if my father was the only one who could vouch for me."

She was not about to point out that this too was not the truth. It left out the small matter of his actually having met Teresa at the cove. These reassurances of Julian's were meaningless. Either she would lie for him, or she would not, and if it was the latter, he would definitely have to come up with another story. Or tell the truth.

"What exactly do you want me to say?" she said.

"That you came to my house after I got home, around 10:15 or 10:30, it's okay to not be quite sure. That you stayed with me nearly till dawn."

"I could tell them I took my bike so Mom wouldn't wonder where I'd gone in the car when she got home."

"Yeah, definitely, the bike. They asked me how you got to my house and I said I didn't know." He pulled her close again. "I knew I could count on you."

The words stung. Partly because she wasn't certain he could count on her. And because she didn't know if she could count on him ever again.

"I need to go," he said. "The cops told me not to leave the house. I gotta sneak in there before they come back."

"Cassie?" Her mother's tremulous voice made them jump back from each other.

Standing at the barn door, her mother wore a raincoat with water dripping from the hood. She stared at Julian, and it was not a good stare. Her gaze shifted to Cassie. "I need to talk to you."

"Hi, Mrs. Moran. I was just leaving," he said. Then to Cassie: "Call you tonight." He hurried past her mother, who was looking daggers at him now.

"What is it?" Cassie said.

Her mother checked behind her, waiting till he was out of earshot. "The police just called. They're sending someone over to ask you some questions."

"What about?"

"They wouldn't say. But word's getting around Julian might be involved. The police were at his house today."

"He didn't do anything," Cassie said.

Her mother grasped her arm as she tried to leave the barn. "I want you to tell them the truth. If he's involved, you can't protect him. You mustn't try to protect him."

Cassie gave her an angry look, taking back her arm and continuing through the rain toward the house. Steeling herself for the next part.

Chapter Five

CASSIE HAD NOT ACTUALLY TOLD Julian she would lie for him, and she still hadn't made up her mind. If he turned out to be the killer and her lie saved him, or if he was innocent and her telling the truth convicted him… in either case she would never forgive herself. Damned if you do, damned if you don't.

The police were due to arrive any minute. She felt like she needed someone or something to help her come to a decision, but she simply had no time. There wasn't any point in discussing it with her mother, who'd already made her opinion clear. Cassie was to tell the truth no matter what.

Grant Wolcott came to mind. He'd asked her if she was still seeing Julian and seemed surprised when she said she was. Maybe he knew something about Julian and Teresa.

She darted up the steps to use the extension in her mother's bedroom where she could speak privately. She'd never gotten an extension in her room, much to her unhappiness in high school. Pulling out the directory from under the phone, she scanned through it for the Wolcott's number, but there wasn't a separate listing for the guesthouse.

With little time remaining, she called the main house. It must've been a maid or housekeeper who answered and gave her the number for the cottage. She banged down the phone and dialed again.

Outside, a car door slammed shut. The police were here, she was out of time.

"Hello?" Grant said on the phone.

"Grant? This is Cassie Moran." She kept her voice low as the doorbell rang and her mother went to answer it. "I have to ask you something. You seemed surprised when I said I was still with Julian. Was there a reason for that? Do you know anything I don't know?"

He went silent for a minute. Meanwhile, her mother called up from downstairs. "Cassie, come down please!"

She cupped the phone and shouted toward the door. "I just got out of the shower. Be there in a sec!" Her mother would know she was lying, but wouldn't tell the police.

Grant was speaking again. "I didn't want to say anything. It wasn't really my business. But yeah, I saw him with Teresa Patterson a couple weeks ago. At Thorne Cove, in fact. They were making out."

Her mouth grew dry. Though their cars parked at the cove had been damning, this was the first eyewitness account that confirmed their relationship.

"It looks bad for him, I know," Grant said. "But I can't believe he had anything to do with what happened. I'm sure you feel the same."

"Of course," she whispers. "Hey thanks, I gotta go." She felt like she'd been hit by a truck. Until now, she'd been able to maintain a smidgeon of doubt. Like, maybe that hadn't been Teresa's car at the cove. Or maybe it was, but someone else had borrowed it. Or maybe it was her car, and she was the one who'd driven it to the cove, but it was just a coincidence Julian stopped there at the same time. He always liked late night swims.

But now she knew for certain they really had been seeing each other. No matter how hard she tried to make excuses for him, she couldn't anymore.

"Cassie! Officer Brooks is waiting to speak with you!" her mother shouted.

"Coming!" Dread filled her as she made her way down the stairs.

A young man in uniform, probably no more than twenty-five, stood in the hallway. On seeing her, he smiled and extended his hand. "Hi Cassie. I'm Officer Brooks." She could understand right away why he'd been picked to come talk to her. His handshake was firm and reassuring. His voice conveyed warmth; his face was wholesome. He looked like the boy scout who helped grannies cross the street, all grown up. She liked him instantly.

"I remember your dad," he said. "He coached my Little League team for two years. What a nice man. I didn't have much talent for the sport, but he made me feel like I really made a difference on the team."

"Thanks, yeah, he was like that." If she wasn't already feeling like this guy was on her side, this would've been it. How could she feel hostile toward someone who admired her dead father?

He turned to her mother. "Mrs. Moran, I'd like to speak to her privately if that's all right."

Cassie's mother looked at her. "Is it okay with you?"

She hesitated before nodding. Since she was over eighteen, the officer could probably insist if he wanted. She wasn't a child who required a parent present.

They went into the kitchen while her mother headed upstairs to her room. "Do you want something to drink?" Cassie said.

"No thanks. Have a seat."

She poured herself a glass of water while he got out a notepad. They settled at the table. "This shouldn't take very long. I want to reassure you that you're not a suspect here. We just need to corroborate someone else's statement with you."

"All right."

He grew somber. "I'm sure you must've heard what happened to Teresa Patterson."

She nodded, not trusting herself to speak.

"Well, in the process of investigating the case, your name came up. So I'm going to ask you to tell me your whereabouts last night. Is that okay?"

Her hands were starting to tremble. She clasped them together under the table. "Sure."

"But before you start, I want to say something. I know what it's like to be your age and maybe in love, right? Not so long since I was the same age. And I know what it's like to want to protect the person you care for."

He paused and scratched his chin. "But the fact is, it's always, always better to go with the truth. If the person you want to protect is innocent, the truth is their best defense. It may not always seem that way, but trust me on this. When someone is lying, it's generally easy for us to figure out. But it leaves us thinking, why did she lie, right? So the person she's protecting might be innocent, but we're left wondering if they're guilty because of the lie.

"On the other hand, if the person you want to protect is guilty, you definitely don't want to lie for them. In this case, the guilty person has committed murder. I'm sure you don't want a murderer to get away with the crime. People who commit violence of any sort will commit violence again. Believe me, I've studied this. You don't want to feel responsible for anyone else getting hurt or killed in the future.

"And lastly, think of Teresa's family. There's nothing worse than losing a child, or a sister, and knowing the killer got away with it. Her family deserves justice. You can help them just by telling the truth.

"This was my long-winded way of asking you to tell me where you were last night starting at around seven p.m."

She had never been so torn regarding any decision before. She hated Julian for putting her in this situation. But he was also the sun and earth and sea to her. Could he possibly have killed Teresa, or any woman? Although he'd cheated on her, she still couldn't believe the boy she knew so well might've murdered someone.

She was aware her hesitation to respond made it increasingly clear she was considering a lie. An unconvincing lie would be worse than not lying as far as Julian's situation was concerned.

Grant's words echoed inside her and hardened her heart: *I saw him with Teresa Patterson.* Still, when she opened her mouth, she wasn't certain what would come out of it until the words began. "I was home alone till about eleven last night. Then I went out on my bike." She explained how her mother had gone straight to bed after returning from the party.

"Is there a reason you didn't take the car?"

"I like riding at night." She added the part about her mother possibly getting worried if she heard the car start.

"Okay. Where did you go?"

"I took Ocean Avenue, planning to go to Julian's. I wanted to avoid traffic. But on the way…" Here was where she hesitated. She swallowed a lump and blurted out the rest.

"I saw his truck parked along the side of the road. Right before the turnoff to Thorne Cove."

"Are you certain it was Julian's truck?"

"You know how there's a lobster painted on the back? I did that."

"Got it, okay. Please continue."

"I slowed and looked down the lane. I saw another car I thought I recognized. A rusty green VW Bug. I wasn't sure, but I thought it was Teresa's car."

"She does have a vehicle of that description. Did you see the license number?"

She shook her head. "It was dark. And it wouldn't have occurred to me to even look at it."

"Okay. You saw the car. Do you know what time it was then? Did you check your watch?"

"I wasn't wearing one. I think it was a little after eleven."

"Fair enough," he said. "Looking down the lane, did you see Teresa or Julian?"

"No. Neither one of them."

"Did you go to the cove?"

She shook her head again. "I turned my bike around and went home."

"Was there a reason you didn't go look for Julian at the cove? I mean, you were on your way to see him anyway."

She blew out a heavy breath. "Well, it was because of Teresa's car. It made me think he was going to meet her. It made me upset. That's why I went home."

"So you didn't see her there either?"

"No. I saw Julian's truck and Teresa's car, then I turned around and went back home. That's it."

"Did you have any other reason to suspect Julian was seeing her?"

She considered saying what Grant had just told her on

the phone. But she decided against it, mainly because this wasn't knowledge she had at the time. "I saw her hanging around near Julian's house yesterday morning. And he acted a little funny, like he wasn't sure about us… our relationship. I thought it was strange he would've planned a night out with his friends on the day he knew I'd be back from college."

"Is there anything else you'd like to tell me?"

Her eyes filled with tears. "Officer, I can't believe Julian would ever hurt anyone. I've dated him for years and he's always been as gentle as can be. He could never kill a person. He's innocent. He has to be."

After finishing his notes, Officer Brooks stood and offered her a tissue. "Thank you for telling me the truth, Cassie. I hope you're right about Julian."

As soon as he was gone, her mother returned to the kitchen. Cassie wept hot tears on her shoulder.

Chapter Six

AFTER BETRAYING the boy she loved, she could think of nothing further to do. Her mother wanted her to talk about it when she was done crying, but she turned away from her, went up the stairs, crawled into bed, and pulled the covers over herself. This was no more effective in erasing the horror of the last twenty-four hours than if she were a turtle drawing her head inside her shell.

The weather was going downhill fast, mirroring the day's events. The wind wheezed through narrow gaps in the windows. Rain pelted the glass. Branches beat the side of their house.

Her thoughts settled into two distinct camps that lay siege upon each other. In corner number one she reassured herself she'd done the right thing in telling the truth. If her boyfriend was a killer she would not—must not—protect him with a lie.

But corner number two did not believe Julian capable of hurting anyone, let alone murdering them. Therefore she should've lied to save him from the appearance of guilt that would surely be used against him even if he were innocent.

A knock put an end to the debate and caused her to poke her head out from under the sheet. Her mother opened the door without waiting for a reply. "Officer Brooks just called. He wanted to know if Julian came here after he left."

"They don't know where Julian is?"

She shook her head.

Cassie sprang from the bed and crossed to the window. Darkness had settled in, but the front house lights illuminated sheets of rain ricocheting off the roof of their car, and the maple sapling bent so low by the force of the gale, it looked like it would snap. "I have to go."

"Stay here, Cassie. It's a nor'easter out there."

"I'll be careful." She slipped into her sneakers and dashed past her mother, trying to ignore her stricken expression. Downstairs she paused to find the car keys under the newspaper on the counter.

Few other motorists were foolish enough to be on the road. She drove too fast into a deep pool and nearly slid into a ditch before connecting with the solid surface again. When she neared Julian's house, she glimpsed police cars lined up out front. She parked in the first stretch of empty space and the rain drenched her as she rushed along the sidewalk, splattering through puddles. Officer Brooks was in his squad car but he nodded to another cop to let her into the house.

Julian's father emerged from the kitchen, walking with bent shoulders and a shuffling step. Seeing Cassie, he said, "You gonna catch your death of cold." He disappeared into the back and returned with a towel. "Dry off."

"Where is he?" she said.

"He took the boat." His eyes glistened as he shifted his gaze to the window. "They called the Coast Guard."

Her arms started shaking and she pulled the towel tight around them. "Why would he do that?"

Armando lowered his voice. "My boy lost hope. The cops searched, said we had a knife missin' from our set in the kitchen. The murder weapon, they said. We told them anyone coulda taken it. When do we ever lock our doors?"

The image of Teresa with a bloody knife wound made her shudder. "What can we do?" she said.

"Wait. And pray. Never helped me before but maybe God in heaven been savin' up for this." Armando crossed the room to where a photograph of Julian's teenage mother rested on the mantle. She had only been seventeen when she died. He kissed the tips of his fingers and pressed them against her face before lifting the rosary that hung over the frame. Holding it, he lowered his head, muttering words in Portuguese.

Cassie stared through the front window at angry waves crashing against the sea wall across the street. If she'd thought her prayers would make any difference, she still would not have been able to decide whether to pray for his escape, or for his safe return into the arms of the police waiting to arrest him.

Part Two: Witch

CASSIE (AGE 26)

Chapter Seven

CASSIE RIDES her bike back from work on one of those rare June afternoons when the sky is blue, the breeze light, and the humidity low. This perfection of elements brings on a feeling close to happiness.

As usual, Gio begins meowing before she opens the door. When she walks in, he tangles himself between her legs, immediately under foot. She wishes she could believe her mere presence fills him with joy, but clearly the amount of attention she receives depends on how urgently he requires her services at the moment.

After putting away her purse, she feeds the poor starving beast. He gulps down his food in chunks with an enthusiasm she envies. How much simpler life would be if the highlight of everyone's day was merely dinner.

Her cat follows her out the back door and plops on the brick patio to clean himself, while she arranges the lawn sprinkler and turns it on. A few drops reach Gio, causing him to leap backward, shaking off his fur while throwing her an affronted look.

She unravels the hose to water the rhododendrons, which are looking wilted. They've had two weeks without rain and she's trying her best not to let anything die on her watch. Her mother has been more than generous, leaving the place in her hands when she moved to Florida last year. Cassie only has to cover taxes and utilities. The house and the old red barn could both use some repairs, which she plans to do after she saves up enough money.

When she's finished with the plants, she brings in the mail—bills and catalogues—and tosses it into the pile on the table by the door. For dinner, she cooks herself brown rice and stir-fried veggies with cheese. Simple but healthy and it generally tastes good enough, depending on which vegetables she happens to have on hand. By the time she brings her meal into the family room to eat in front of the nightly news, Gio has positioned himself at the foot of her chair, ready to snatch falling particles. He carries inside him a deep well of hope that never dries out.

Since it's June, she still has an hour and a half till sunset after she's finished doing the dishes. Gio trots after her to the studio in the barn, and curls into his cozy bed by the door while she gets out her supplies. She uses acrylics because they're easier to clean than oils, especially when her cat manages to spread wet paint all over himself.

Currently on her canvas she's depicted a woman with long auburn hair walking into the woods. Over the past few days, the painting has taken on more and more of an ominous feel, she's not sure why. Maybe because the forest is growing darker, and the branches of the trees are starting to look like the arms and hands of skeletons. The woman faces away from the viewer, something that's true of all Cassie's work. She loves the mystery of it, letting you imagine what her face might look like.

When the sun dips low and the sky turns crimson, she calls Gio, who has disappeared and is probably hunting mice in the bushes. He comes right away, not wanting to be left behind, even though he can return whenever he wants through his cat door.

The phone rings before they're inside, and she's pretty certain she knows who it is. Grant Wolcott. He moved back from Philadelphia a month earlier, after earning his MBA from Wharton and then working at an investment firm for several years. Since his return, they've had coffee a few times, though she has mixed feelings about renewing their acquaintance. This is why she doesn't rush to answer. However, since it's still ringing when she finally reaches the kitchen extension, she decides to pick up.

"Hope I'm not calling too late," he says.

She can't tell if he's being serious or not, and it makes her wonder if he knows what a pathetic life she leads. If he'd called twenty minutes later, he really would've been too late.

"It's fine, I was just painting," she says.

"Good. I was wondering if you want to go out on the boat with me tomorrow. Do some fishing, go for a swim, putter around the coast. Whatever you like."

Until now she'd forgotten tomorrow is Saturday. She racks her brain for an excuse because this sounds like a date and she hasn't dated anyone in a long time. She's not sure she wants to start up again, particularly not with Grant. It isn't that she has anything against him, but she's afraid being around him will bring back all the memories.

Still, the weather is supposed to be beautiful again tomorrow and she suddenly misses being out on a boat larger than her canoe. Before she can stop herself, words are coming out of her mouth: "Sure. Forget the fishing. The rest sounds good." They agree on a time before hanging up.

She stands by the phone a moment longer, hoping she hasn't made a mistake. It's just a boat ride, she tells herself. It's not a promise to get married and bear his children. It's not even an agreement to have sex with him.

Before going to sleep, she watches a dumb sci-fi movie with aliens. Probably because the meteorite that fell behind her hedges also came from outer space, she's reminded she still hasn't done anything about it. If she does decide to contact the science museum, it will have to wait till Monday now.

Recalling the way the thing sparked her, she checks her arm. It's only been a day, but the mark has disappeared entirely. There isn't any pain when she touches it either. Clearly it wasn't anything to be concerned about.

Gio follows her to bed and snuggles beside her. Her thoughts turn to Julian, as they often do. She remembers their night together before she left for college. One of their last happy moments.

She thinks she's about to drift asleep when suddenly her head heats up like a match was lit inside it. Sweat pops out of her forehead and the back of her neck. She opens her eyes but sees only blackness. The bed seems to drop out from under her and she's falling, falling, falling into a limitless void.

Chapter Eight

CASSIE'S BODY jolts as it settles back on the firm surface of the bed again. The burning sensation in her head subsides. Her vision returns but she can't believe what she sees.

It isn't her bed, or even her room. She's wrapped in Julian's arms, lying on his bed, in his room. It has to be a dream, yet it feels exactly as if she's awake and living in the moment.

"Cass?" Julian's breath tickles her ear, his voice soft and low as she remembers it.

She's afraid if she looks at him her heart will explode. She's afraid if she doesn't, the dream will end and he'll disappear.

"You okay?" he says.

She doesn't say anything because this isn't real. But when seconds pass without any change in her perceptions, she lifts her face to him. His rich brown eyes filled with concern make her lose it. Tears gush as she draws back from him, at the same time grasping his shoulders and shaking as hard as she can. The sheet falls down, exposing her nakedness, which she assumes is all part of the dream.

"Why, Julian? Why did you do it?" She continues to cry out *why* in a frenzy, not even knowing whether the question is *why did you cheat* or *why did you kill her?*

Julian's arms fold around her and hold her tight until she calms down, gulping in air. "Do what?" he says in a gentle voice. "What did I do?"

"You didn't love me enough." Her answer is petulant, like a child pouting to her mother. It doesn't begin to encapsulate an answer to his question, but she doesn't want to get into it when this is only a dream.

"That isn't true." He kisses her hair. "You're feeling bad because you're leaving. But I'll be here when you get back. You know? Waiting for you. Nothing's gonna happen to us."

A bitter laugh gets stuck in the back of her throat at the irony. She pulls up the sheet to cover herself and wipes her eyes with it. "I've never had a dream as real as this before."

"Dream?" His head tilts the way it always did when he was puzzled. A movement that endears him to her.

"Either that or I'm losing my mind." She presses her hand against his cheek. "Your face is warm. I've never dreamt with all my senses before." She sniffs the air beside him. "There's mint on your breath. Your clock is making a buzzing noise. I'm seeing details I don't even remember, like the way it's torn at the corner of your Jethro Tull poster."

"Don't joke. Not tonight." When he rolls over and stands up, she's shocked to see he's naked too. It makes sense though. On this night long ago, they made love. But since when did a dream make sense?

He pulls on cotton pants before retrieving a small box from his desk drawer. "Got you something." He takes her hand and places it on her palm.

She shifts her gaze between the expectant look in his eyes, and the box, feeling compelled to play along. Of course, she knows what the gift will be, but when she opens it, she acts surprised just to please him. "Thank you," she whispers, holding back more tears.

He takes out the silver band and slips it on the third finger of her right hand. "It's not good enough to be an engagement ring. But it's my promise to be faithful."

"Don't make promises you can't keep." Though he deserves this rebuke, she regrets it as soon as she sees the hurt in his eyes.

"You don't believe me?"

"It's going to be hard."

"Will you be faithful to me?"

"Always," she says.

"So will I." He sits beside her, resting his arm on her shoulder. She remains perfectly still, not wanting anything to interrupt the dream.

"Don't be sad. Only three months till Christmas. You'll be back in no time," he says.

It feels so real she almost wonders if everything that's happened since this day is the actual dream from which she has only just awoken. A sharp urgency fills her.

"Run away with me," she says. "Tonight. We'll go somewhere else, start a new life together."

"You don't mean that."

"I do. I've got some money. It'll hold us till we find work."

Julian is silent. He must think she's lost her mind. Then he says, "You're going to college. You can't give up on that."

"I'll give up anything so we can be together. I will." Again that stubborn, childish note in her voice.

"I can't leave my father. He needs my help on the boat."

"He'll have to hire someone when you go to the conservatory."

"That's at least a year away, if it even happens. I need to save up more money first." His eyes light up with excitement as he gets on his knees in front of her. He places his hand under her chin and makes her look at him. "Ask me what my goals are."

"Why don't you just tell me?"

"C'mon."

"Okay. What are your goals?"

"Number three, make a living even if it means I have to keep catching lobsters."

"What's number one?"

"Getting there. Number two, become a world-renowned pianist. I don't know if I can support myself that way. That's why I need number three."

"If you're world-renowned, someone ought to pay you," she says.

"And number one… make Cassie Moran happy."

She lowers her forehead to his shoulder. "You really mean that?" This is her mind playing with her, saying what she wants to hear.

"You and me forever, Cass." He taps his heart with his fist. Then he's back on his feet. "You should go now. It's late."

In her memory, she was the one to say it was time for her to go. But dreams don't follow scripts, she reminds herself. On this night—their last before she left for Syracuse—they only made love once, but what's to stop them from doing it again inside her dream? And if they do, will it be as achingly beautiful as it was the time before?

But he's handing her clothes to her and she lets the moment pass. After she dresses, he takes her hand and they tiptoe down the stairs. They don't want to wake his father, sleeping in his room at the back of the house.

The front door creaks when Julian opens it, exactly as it did that night. Then and now, Armando does not get up and she remembers feeling sure that even if he were awake, he would have no intention of disturbing them. They go out to the front yard where Julian wraps her in his arms and kisses her again. "Don't let me go," she whispers, clinging to him. He pulls back a bit but she refuses to release him.

It's no use, though. Her head grows hot as her vision blackens. Julian's fading form leaves a hollow space between her arms.

Chapter Nine

THE MORNING after her vivid dream, Cassie wakes at nine feeling well-rested. She supposes that means the sequence flashed by in a second of dream time, and she spent the rest of the night sleeping deeply.

Still, the experience has left her unsettled. When she climbs out of bed, she unearths the box of Julian mementos from her closet for the first time in several years and opens it up. She digs through its contents till she finds the silver ring—now tarnished—and puts it on. Its size, its weight, and the way it fits her finger are exactly what she remembers from the dream. How did her subconscious recall it so accurately?

Gio is meowing, the sign that breakfast is past due. She replaces the ring, goes downstairs in her pajamas, and prepares him a mixture of canned food and kibble. She makes scrambled eggs for herself and places the morning newspaper before her on the table, hoping it will keep her from dwelling on how disturbing it was to experience that night with Julian again in such rich detail.

The front page includes an article on the meteor shower,

and she skims it to see if anyone else reported finding one or receiving a spark from it. No one did.

None of the other news catches her interest, no matter how long she stares at the headlines. Considering the day ahead of her, she regrets agreeing to join Grant on his boat. She's quite sure she won't make good company while she's still trying to wrap her head around what happened last night. On the other hand, getting out of the house may be the best way to force these troubling thoughts from her mind.

Upstairs, she puts on her newest bikini and models it in front of the mirror. Her thighs look flabby, but what else is new? It's best if she's not overly beguiling anyway. After covering up with her favorite sundress, she brushes her hair and considers a ponytail. Better to leave it loose since she'll be swimming, she decides. She applies pale lipstick and eye shadow though it'll get washed away soon enough. Not that she's trying to wow him with her looks, but it seems more respectful to put in at least the minimum of effort.

Before leaving she reminds Gio to be a good boy. A few days ago, he was not a good boy when he dragged a small dead bird into the house through his cat door. She doubts he learned his lesson, though.

Since today's forecast promised the same clear skies and not-stiflingly-hot temperatures as yesterday, she takes her bicycle. Passing through the small downtown, she notices a new shop called "Broom Witch Antiques," an obvious play on the town's name of Brumewich.

Though many make fun of it, Cassie loves their town name. *Brume* means *fog* or *mist* and does not refer to a device used for sweeping (or flying across the sky). *Wich* is just a common ending for towns in New England. But people think of witches when they see the name. It's understandable, given

Massachusetts' sordid history of persecuting innocent women for no good reason whatsoever.

In fact the idea of witchcraft has always intrigued her. As a child, she constantly drew herself as a witch. She would be soaring across the sky on her broomstick and striking the people below with her lightning spells. These would never permanently harm anyone but might turn them into a bug or a snake for a little while. Or she might cause a person's hair to turn green, or their hands to sprout a sixth finger, or their heads to face their backsides. She had nice spells too, that would help an awkward or homely girl or boy to find friendship and love. Spells that changed bullies into saints and struggling students into future Einsteins. Her witch fantasy gave her the sensation of power and maybe that was all it was ever about.

Drawing near the Wolcott manor, she can't help marveling again at its perfection. Of course, with that kind of money, they can afford to keep the place up. If the paint peels in one spot, reason enough to have the whole mansion redone. As opposed to her house, where they had to wait till the paint hung in ragged patches all over before calling every painter in the area to try to get the best price.

She follows the driveway to the guesthouse entrance. Grant has been staying here since his return from Philadelphia. Most twenty-nine-year-old men would not want to be living back home with Mommy—his father passed away five years ago—but he'd have to pay a fortune in rent to get something half as nice minus all the amenities. She doubts his mother charges him anything, though one never knows with the rich. Sometimes they're far stingier than those who have nothing. She imagines that's how they become those-who-have-everything.

Grant calls to her from the dock. As she approaches along

the path between the two houses, he pauses to watch her. "You look pretty."

"Thanks." She always feels awkward when anyone compliments her. If she says something nice in return, it comes across that she's being polite, not genuine. Instead, she changes the subject. "Is this new?" She nods at the shiny white-and-blue Boston Whaler, just the right size for vrooming along the coast with a few friends.

"We've had it a while," Grant says.

She's noticed he likes to downplay their wealth and she likes that about him. His mother, on the contrary, never lets anyone forget her money places her well above them in the town pecking order.

Before long they untie from the dock and head out along the channel toward open water. "Where are we going?" she asks, not that it matters. It's enough just to be out on the water, with the sun heating her and the fine mist on her face.

"I thought we might go by the lighthouse. It's high tide." He says this because Farer's Light marks Farer's Ledge, a cluster of black rocks situated just below the surface of the ocean some distance from their shore. The ledge sank many ships in the mid-1800s, before the lighthouse was built. At high tide, though, they can motor over the rocks safely.

"Sure. I haven't seen it up close for a while," she says.

But when they draw near the base of the lighthouse, she feels uneasy. It's an enormous granite structure that looms eighty or ninety feet straight out of the ocean. A ladder runs up the side of it. The part she doesn't like, though, is seeing the rock underneath them, hovering like a massive sea crea-ture preparing to rear up its monstrous back.

When she turns toward Grant, he's looking at her like he's trying to figure something out. But he shifts his gaze quickly, not liking that she's caught him staring, apparently. "When I was a kid, my friends and I used to climb the ladder and jump off," he says. "You ever do that?"

"A few times. I was scared to death looking down from the jumping point, but somehow I managed it."

"A rite of passage."

"Can't call yourself a Brume-witch till then."

He gives her a crooked smile. "I never called myself that."

"What do you say then? Brume wizard?"

"Better," he says.

She's distracted thinking about the time she and Julian took his father's lobsterboat out here. They went up the ladder and got into the lighthouse through a door with a broken lock. Then they made love on an old chair. Later they laughed about it, saying it was the start of crazy places they would have sex. A lighthouse was their first and later it would be a train or an airplane and then maybe they'd do a love-making tour of the national monuments. They went on quite a while thinking of unusual places to do it. As it turned out their list never grew longer than *a lighthouse.*

After a swing round Farer's Light, they go near the beach closest to the harbor and anchor for a swim. Grant dives in while she tests the water with her toe, hanging from the ladder. "How is it?"

"Like there could be ice cubes floating around in here." He swims hard away from the boat and she watches the water ripple over his shoulder blades. She thought he was scrawny in high school, more of a bookish type, but he's grown muscles since then. His father was a tall, distinguished-looking man. Some people called his mother a beauty, but she never saw it. Money buys good opinions along with every-thing else.

Grant returns and splashes her, making her scream. "Chicken!" He dives down and goes under the boat.

She jumps in. The water feels even colder than she expected and she shoots back up, gasping. She launches into a crawl to warm herself. Grant catches up and they race toward the beach. When they can nearly touch bottom, they pause and tread water.

"I suppose you need to be a Brume witch or wizard to get into this ocean," he says.

"Our blood must run cold."

She's starting to feel a connection to Grant. This is their heritage... creatures of the sea, guardians of the coast, witches and wizards of the east. They'll always be of Brumewich.

Wondering if he feels the same, she asks: "Why did you come back from Philadelphia?"

"Why did you come back from Syracuse after college?"

"I asked you first."

His pale eyes look at her in a way that makes her spine tingle. "You know the answer, Cassie." He flips back into the water and swims toward the boat.

Chapter Ten

WHEN THEY GET BACK to the dock Grant asks if she'll have dinner with him. She says she's tired and wants to go home and clean the saltwater off her. It's a lame excuse, but he knows her well enough not to argue. In fact, because he's been nice and hasn't pressed her, she gives him an opening by suggesting they do it another time.

Her evening is a repeat of the night before, and the many nights before that. A simple, nutritious dinner. Two hours working on her painting. Back into the house to cuddle with Gio while reading an Agatha Christie novel. After twenty-five pages, she remembers she's read it before and puts it away.

She's tired yet almost afraid to go to bed. She doesn't want a repeat of last night's photo-realistic dream. On the other hand, she can't simply give up sleeping from now on.

When she does finally slip under the sheet, she tries not to think of Julian at all. This works about as well as one would imagine. She finds her thoughts flooded with memories of him, and before she knows it, she's picturing the day she came home from college for the Christmas holiday.

It happens the same as before, with the inside of her head feeling as if it's boiling over and her vision darkening. Seconds later she gets the tumbling sensation. When she can see again, she's standing on the staircase in her house, about to lose her balance. With one hand, she lunges for the bannister, at the same time banging her leg with the suitcase on her other side.

It's every bit as real as last night's experience, which she hesitates to even call a dream anymore. It was more like a strange sort of time travel, during which she relived an event that happened in the past. But she doesn't have time to analyze it now.

Something metal bangs in the kitchen. She's about to call out "Gio!" when she remembers he isn't even born yet. It has to be her mother. The aroma of Christmas cookies baking in the oven reaches her, waking a gnawing hunger inside her.

She knows exactly when this is. She's just returned from her first semester at Syracuse. She rode back with Sarah and her father, who live in Ruford. Cassie's mother greeted her at the door upon her arrival, before quickly disappearing to tend to the cookies.

"Everything all right, honey?" Her mother peers out at her from the kitchen.

The urge to hug her mother fills Cassie, but she holds back, though she hasn't seen her in six months. It isn't just that she's missed her. This seven-years-younger version of her mother looks so different. Her skin is smoother, her figure thinner, and her hair is still its natural chestnut color. Cassie aches a bit inside thinking how time takes its toll, and how quickly people age.

Again she wonders how all the details are right in this dream or whatever-it-is, including the way her mother would've looked seven years ago.

"I thought I was dreaming," Cassie says.

Her mother smiles. "It must feel like that, coming back home after your first time away." The timer buzzes and she spins around to deal with the cookies.

Cassie continues up the stairs and deposits the suitcase on her bed. Turning on the overhead light, she glimpses her own reflection in the mirror. Last night in the semi-darkness at Julian's house, she had no chance to see what she looked like. Curious, she peers into the glass and is taken back to the era when her dirty blond hair was straighter and fell more than halfway down her back. These days, she's keeping it a little shorter with more of a Stevie Nicks look—bangs and unruly curls. Along with the differences in hair, this girl she's staring at in the mirror has fuller cheeks and whiter skin than her waking self, currently sporting a decent tan. The paleness, however, is consistent with this dream taking place in winter.

Once again, her dream has gotten every detail right. In fact it's nothing like a dream, but exactly what she'd expect if she traveled through time. Except... if she jumped into the past, wouldn't there be two of her now? Time travel in science fiction stories had people running into their younger or older selves. This would create a paradox so confusing she could never quite wrap her head around the explanation. But that was how it was supposed to work. In this case, though, she *is* the younger version of herself. If it's time travel, it's for the mind only. She left her future body at home.

When the doorbell rings downstairs, her mother gets it. A second later she shouts up, "Cassie, Julian's here!"

She closes her eyes and breathes in slowly to calm herself. *It's just a dream.* Except it's nothing like a dream.

Her feet move her to the top of the stairs. Julian looks up from the bottom with particles of snow on his wool beanie and light reflecting in his eyes. This is all it takes. Excitement overwhelms her and sends her flying down the steps into his arms. "I missed you so much," he says into her ear.

"Missed you too." It's true, even counting last night's rendezvous. Part of her wants to drag him back upstairs and into her bed, but it would be awkward with her mother in the kitchen making them cookies.

"How was it?" Julian says.

"How was what?"

He laughs at her. "Um, that place you were. What's it called? College?"

She's already forgotten she's just come from there on this day in the past. "Oh let's not talk about that." Through the front window, she glimpses white powder settling on the driveway. "Let's go outside." She tells her mother they're going for a walk as she throws on a coat, mittens, and a hat. Aside from gloves, Julian has only his jean jacket over a sweater, but this is typical of him. A true child of New England, he was never one to get cold or hot but somehow his internal temperature always balances between the extremes of winter and summer.

Before leaving, she ducks into the kitchen to grab four warm cookies, handing two to Julian. After scarfing them down, they go to the barn to fetch the toboggan, which he pulls along the slick road on their way to the sledding hill. They pass the haunted house, which is what they used to call the Quinn place. A heavy dose of nostalgia hits her to see its broken shutters, cracked glass, and peeling paint. A few years after this, someone will buy the house and modernize it, destroying its mystery and allure.

Julian pretends to stop for something and next thing she knows, a snowball smashes into her shoulder.

"You're gonna pay for that, Reis." She dashes to the nearest snowbank and scoops up a handful, patting it into shape. When she turns back, he's coming at her, but she gets him right in the side of his head.

"Oh, you wanna play dirty?" he says, aiming one at her neck. When it hits, the icy particles get under her collar and set off something inside her. She gathers an armful of snow and runs at him with it, knocking him backward into the snowbank, jumping on top of him, and pressing it hard into his face. He's choking, trying to push her away, when she realizes she's gone too far and rolls off him. "Sorry."

He sits up, picking the snow off his face. "What was that about?" He's more confused than pissed, as she can tell from the tilt of his head.

"I didn't mean it." Though actually she did mean it. When it comes to her feelings about Julian, there's something dark and unpredictable lurking just beneath the surface inside her.

"This is me. I know you," he says.

"Okay, I was angry."

"A little snow never set you off like that before. C'mon. Tell me."

She has to remind herself it's a dream. "You make me want to love you, but it isn't real. I don't know you, not really. I can't trust you."

He leans forward, takes her chin with his gloved hand, and turns her face toward him. "You can trust me. Always. I swear it."

His eyes convince her. Despite everything that will happen, she finds herself nodding at him.

"You and me forever, Cass." He taps his heart with his fist like he did before at his house.

She nods again.

"Come on then." He pulls her up into his arms and they continue to the hill, where no one else is around due to the late hour. By the light of a lonely streetlamp, they shoot down the slope over and over, taking turns who's in front and who's in back holding the other tight around the waist. At last, overwhelmed by exhaustion, they crash and spill out of the toboggan. They lie where they fell, making snow angels and sticking out their tongues to catch the falling flakes, until Julian gets on top of her and kisses her with his cold wet lips. She's filled with a sensation of lightness like she hasn't felt since before the murder.

As her head starts heating and spinning, she cries out and clutches him harder, but nothing she does can stop this perfect moment from ending right now.

Chapter Eleven

AS ON THE PREVIOUS NIGHT, Cassie recalls nothing further till she wakes in the morning. Sunlight streams through her window and Gio is standing on her chest meowing into her face. Feeling slightly less rested than she did yesterday, she gets up to feed him.

While he eats, she sits at the kitchen table thinking. Two experiences now, each as lifelike as the other. *What's happening to me? Am I losing my mind?* She can't call it dreaming anymore. Dreams aren't precise re-creations of the past.

Time travel. She can't believe she's even considering this, but no other explanation fits. Each occurrence was exactly as if her consciousness had left her present self and leapt backward in time, landing inside her past self.

However, she's not simply reliving events as they played out then. She can change them; she can act differently than she did the first time. The others—Julian and her mother—behave according to how she remembers, though they also vary from the script when prompted by her.

It's too soon—way too soon—to start wondering if she can change the past, and if those changes will propagate to the present. Would she even know that things were different if those changes became her new reality? She shuts off that line of thinking before her head starts to hurt.

As crazy as this idea sounds, she tries to consider it rationally. Something changed in her two days ago. Her gaze shifts to the window as she recalls the meteorite. The mark on her skin hasn't returned; everything looks and feels completely normal. But a horrifying thought occurs. What if a microscopic alien got inside her and is moving her around through time? She folds her arms tight across her stomach, trying to quell the notion.

The arrival of the meteorite is the only unusual event she can remember happening before her dreams began. Feeling she ought to take a closer look at it in the daylight, she rises and heads for the front yard. Her queasiness increases as another idea comes to her. Maybe it only pretended to be a rock. Maybe it has now wandered off to hide in her house and later emerge in a much more frightening form when she least expects it. Like the baby in *Alien* that grew into full-sized monster in no time at all.

Relief floods her when she peers behind the hedge. The rock is still a rock and hasn't moved from where she left it. She's about to pick it up when she decides she's not being nearly cautious enough. Returning to the house, she fetches her wool jacket, oven mitts, and a cardboard box. Anyone would think she was nuts armoring herself like this to pick up a little stone, but she doesn't want to be sparked again. However, nothing at all happens when she places the meteorite in the box.

She doesn't want the thing inside the house with her, but

she thinks she's okay with storing it in the barn. Sticking it on a shelf in the back, she covers the box with a heavy piece of wood. *Try climbing out of that.* But if it really is an alien that somehow arrived here from light years away, she doubts her little box is going to stymie it.

Chapter Twelve

BECAUSE IT'S Sunday and she may be losing her mind, Cassie is spending the day painting. If she truly is going batshit crazy, she ought to be able to come up with something great or at least unique and memorable. She believes a fine line exists between creativity and insanity. Like Van Gogh with the ear, and Munch who painted the screaming woman. She doesn't know if Munch was nuts or not, but the brain that envisioned an image like that could not exactly be stable.

It's the third cloudless day in a row, but unlike before, it's become uncomfortably hot and the humid air is stifling. Her T-shirt and shorts are sticking to her. She has the sliding barn door fully open to try to catch a breeze, but hasn't felt any yet. She adjusts her position so at least she won't be standing in the sun.

After staring at her painting of a girl in the woods for several minutes, she realizes she's not in the mood for it. She takes it down from her easel and sets it aside before going to the shelf where she stores the records and tapes she likes to listen to while she's working. As she flips through, her eyes are drawn to Julian's recording of *Rêverie*, which she hasn't played for a long time. Before she can talk herself out of it, she snatches it up and inserts it in the cassette player.

The haunting notes wash over her as she takes out her charcoal and begins sketching. Her hand moves with a surge of energy, and the image of Julian's face that's stuck inside her head starts to form on the paper. Letting her instincts take over, she works like a speed-chess player, drawing whatever snaps into her mind without hesitation.

She's on her third sketch of Julian and fourth time playing the song when a rustling sound by the barn door makes her start and look up.

"Hey Cassie." Grant is leaning against the frame, looking so comfortable she wonders how long he's been there. It's disconcerting that he might've been watching her mad creative frenzy. Immediately she reaches over and shuts off the cassette player. She's not sure he'd have any idea that was Julian playing the piano, but he might.

Worse, she can't let him see these pictures. He'll think she's obsessed with someone she should've jettisoned from her brain years ago.

"Oh hi. You took me by surprise. Did you try to call first? Usually I hear the phone from here." This is a lie. Especially if she has music on, an ambulance could pass by with its sirens blaring and she wouldn't notice. But she's babbling, trying to divert his attention while she closes her sketchpad.

"I hope I didn't frighten you." He doesn't answer her question, which she assumes means he didn't call. *Why would he?* By now he must know her well enough to understand he has a better chance of seeing her if he simply arrives at her door, rather than asking her permission first.

"Can I see it?" He nods toward her sketchpad.

"Too soon. I only just started it. Still needs a lot of work."

He steps toward her. "That's okay. I bet it's better than you think." He reaches toward her pad.

She presses her hand down on the cover. "No really. I'll be embarrassed." She turns toward the canvas she set aside. "Can I get your opinion on this?"

But when she looks back, she finds he's seized the sketchpad and lifted its cover. As he stares down at Julian's face, his grip tightens on the paper and his jaw goes rigid.

"I asked you not to look at it," she says.

"Why in hell would you draw him?" His voice scratches.

She takes back the pad. "It's none of your business."

He tries to play down his annoyance. "You have to admit, this is strange."

"I knew you'd react like this."

"Okay. Sure. I guess I shouldn't have insisted."

Since he's being reasonable now, she softens. "I've had some disturbing dreams lately. When that happens, I need to draw to get it out of me. It's a form of therapy."

"What do you think is causing them?"

She shrugs, not about to bring up the meteorite that sparked her. "Bad memories." Another lie. The memories she's been having are the good ones.

He glances around the barn. "Maybe you ought to get out more."

She gives him a half-smile. "Maybe."

He's sounding more relaxed again. His eyes go to her canvas and she moves aside to let him have a full view of it. Her anger over his seeing the Julian picture is subsiding. He seems to understand now.

He takes a moment to really look at her painting. "Nice," he says.

She's glad he doesn't gush. Gushing never sounds sincere to her.

"I like the colors," he goes on. "And the trees are quite good. Not that I'm any judge. But those branches. Wow. I wouldn't want to walk through that forest."

She uses a damp cloth to wipe the charcoal off her hands. "Thanks."

"Have you tried getting your work into galleries?"

"I don't think it's good enough."

"You won't know unless you try," he says. "My mother could help you. She has a lot of connections."

"I wouldn't want her to feel obligated." She can't imagine her wanting to promote the work of a local-bookstore-clerk-who-hasn't-even-been-to-art-school to her New York art scene friends.

"Don't be silly. Let me know if you want me to talk to her about it."

"Sure," she says. "So, what's up? What brings you here?"

"A little surprise." He leads her outside to where he's left a cooler, a picnic basket, and a vase filled with a mix of summer flowers on the ground. He hands her the vase. "From our garden."

"Thank you." They smell like a spring day. His thoughtfulness touches her.

"Are you hungry? I brought us a picnic."

"Starved. You're really spoiling me. I could get used to this treatment."

"I hope so."

They carry everything to the table on the brick patio in the back and lay the food out.

"Not being sure what you liked, I brought everything," he tells her.

There are cold cuts, sliced cheeses, lettuce, tomatoes, mayo, mustard, white bread, whole wheat bread, strawberries, raspberries, and grapes. And beautiful China plates for setting it all out.

"Wine?" He pulls a bottle of white from the cooler, and two glasses from the basket.

"Remind me to have you plan all my picnics from now on." Actually, she considers it likely his mother's staff prepared everything, but she's decided to play nice and give him all the credit.

He pours their drinks and they assemble their sandwiches. They arrange themselves with a view of the water, watching a canoe floating by in the distance.

Though Grant has impressed her, she's suspicious as to why he would try this hard to do so. She feels a little like Groucho Marx, who refused to join any club that would have him as a member.

"I thought you would return from Philadelphia married to an heiress," she says.

"Is that what you think of me?"

"I don't mean it in a bad way. I was thinking of someone beautiful and classy, like Grace Kelly."

"I dated a few women. But I didn't fall in love with anyone. What about you? I didn't expect you to be single when I got back."

"I like my independence. I'm free as a bird here. No one to clean up after."

"You have a funny way of looking at things. Not all men are slobs. Not all of us expect our girlfriends or wives to clean up after us."

"No, you have servants for that." Maybe she's being too hard on him. But he's the one who keeps pushing this relationship, or whatever it is between them. If it's going to happen, she wants him to understand what he's in for before it even starts.

"I can't help that I was born into a rich family."

"You're right, I'm not being fair. The rich have their own challenges. Kids that end up unemployable. Alcoholism and drug addiction. At least that's what I've heard. But you're obviously doing well for yourself."

"Thank you for setting such a low bar it makes me look really accomplished."

She laughs, pleased to see he's a good sport and has a sense of humor. "I did mean that about valuing my independence," she says.

"I get it. We're alike in that. I'm only staying at the guesthouse till I find a place of my own. Aside from that, I'm not relying on my mother for anything. I have a good job; I support myself."

He pours more wine into her glass. She's starting to feel it; she doesn't drink alcohol often.

After setting down the bottle, he glances over to the cemetery located just beyond the barn. "No wonder you have nightmares, living next to that," he says.

"It's never bothered me. In fact it's amazing. Have you ever looked through it?"

He shakes his head. "My father isn't buried here. He's at the one on Cedar Street." They had two in town.

She takes his hand and pulls him up. "C'mon, then. You can't live here and not know who's been here before us." She leads him a short way down the road to the entrance. It feels nice enough holding his hand she begins to wonder if things could work between them. But she lets go once they get on the path that winds among the gravestones.

She shows him the Yateses and the Browns, the Thompsons and the Marshalls. These names are still ubiquitous in Brumewich. She shows him those who died in the early 1700s, and others during the next two centuries. She leads him to the angel carvings, the site of the soldier who received the Medal of Honor in the Civil War, and the monument to ninety-three souls shipwrecked on Farer's Ledge in the mid-1800s. "I can't believe you've never been here," she says more than once.

The last place they visit is the one most dear. "Look, my father has a view of the harbor. I like to sit here with him."

They get down on the grass and rest their backs against his headstone. Some people think it's disrespectful to sit on a grave, but Cassie knows her father would approve. Grant's shoulder presses against hers while they watch the birds glide over the glassy surface of the water.

Clouds have darkened the sky by the time they get up to leave. On their way to the gate, she leads him along a section of the path they haven't taken yet. However, as they near one of the newer gravesites, she realizes her mistake. She hopes he doesn't imagine she brought him here on purpose; it's bad enough he caught her obsessing over Julian earlier in the day. But she can't turn back now without making an issue of it.

Cassie can't help looking at what's written on the stone as they pass by: *Teresa Patterson. Cherished Daughter. Beloved Sister.* Nor can she keep herself from sneaking a glance back at Grant to see his reaction. He wears a frozen expression, staring at the writing. But then his hard gaze swings in her direction. She could swear his thoughts are exactly what she feared… that she took him past this particular gravesite intentionally. And he's not happy about it. Not at all.

Later she helps him gather up the picnic things which unfortunately have attracted ants. She wonders if he's expecting her to ask him to come in and stay a while, perhaps even spend the night with her. But she can't do it, not just because of the uncomfortable look he gave her. There's also the chance she might time travel again in spite of herself, and it would be awkward to wake in the morning with Grant beside her and her thoughts full of Julian.

He seems like himself again when he pauses after opening his car door. "Can I take you to dinner tomorrow?"

"Sure," she says, grateful for their mostly pleasant afternoon. "I'd like that." It gives her another day to delay making any decision about him.

Chapter Thirteen

AFTER GRANT LEAVES she starts a jigsaw puzzle. She chooses a picture of skaters on a frozen pond hoping the winter scene will remind her what not-dying-of-the-heat feels like. It's even worse inside than out because their house has no air conditioning. She turns the fan on full blast, but it's just like a furnace blowing sweltering air into her face.

While putting together the edge pieces, she broods over whether she can really travel through time. It seems unbelievable, but she can't deny the evidence of her senses. The only other explanation is that she's lost the ability to distinguish fantasy from reality.

She considers the latter possibility first. *What if my mind has turned to mush?* She would need professional help in that case. She'd have to go to a psychiatrist and get a diagnosis. If she's suffering from hallucinations, the doctor will no doubt want to start medicating her. And if he believes she's a danger to herself or others, he'll want to commit her to an asylum. He would probably need her permission for that. Or her mother's if they judge her too far gone to make rational decisions anymore.

What if, on the other hand, she's truly gained the ability to go back in time? If she tells that to any medical professionals, they won't believe her. They'll order the same treatment for her as if she really has gone mad.

Obviously, she's rooting for time travel over mental illness as the explanation. She decides it's too soon to share her story with anyone. She needs to understand more about how it works first. Maybe after that she'll have a better idea regarding whether it's happening or not.

If it's real, she should be able to change the past. That ought to be something she can put to the test. On the other hand, she wonders if she's being completely irresponsible. There could be thousands of repercussions she can't possibly anticipate. But maybe they'll be good repercussions. Maybe the changes she makes will transform the world into a better place. This sounds like a whole lot of wishful thinking, however.

What it comes down to is that she can't resist. For whatever reason, this power has fallen on her shoulders, and it's up to her to discover its limits. It isn't something she can discuss with another person. The decision is hers alone.

She'll test her abilities tonight. She's already thought about what to do, and ever since it entered her head, she hasn't been able to think of anything else. She *must* do it.

It's all she can do not to jump into bed immediately, but it's too early, the sun hasn't even set. She takes a cold shower and soaks her hair to cool herself. She thinks about eating something, but since she's still stuffed from the afternoon feast, nothing sounds appealing. Instead, she flicks on the TV and switches channels till she finds a boring-sounding documentary. Gio hops onto her lap and they watch it together, although the heat from his small body has perspiration emerging from all her pores again.

After the show ends, she goes up to bed. This time she turns her thoughts to her father, not Julian. Though it's painful to recall, she focuses on their last conversation. Before long she feels the familiar sensations that indicate she's about to tumble into the past.

When her vision clears again, she's in the kitchen staring at her father. Seeing him standing before her—*alive*—fills her with confusion and remorse. But also joy to have this chance to be with him again. Her emotions are so overwhelming her knees buckle and she grabs the edge of the counter to steady herself. Because he never got the chance to age beyond this day, he looks exactly as she remembers him. Pale freckles and sand-colored hair held flat by a generous application of gel. Gentle brown eyes that never looked stern, no matter how hard Cassie provoked him. Like tonight.

She rushes into his arms, startling him. He pats her back. "What's all this? A second ago I was ruining your life."

In reality, that was the last sentence she spoke to him. *You're ruining my life.*

She can change that now. "I didn't mean it, Dad. Forgive me. I love you so much." Her voice sounds girlish. She's her fourteen-year-old self—shorter, and with smaller breasts.

He kisses her cheek. "I know you didn't mean it. Love you too." When he draws back, she notices the crisp blue suit he wears. He's going to Boston for a mandatory event organized by his company. "Take care of your mother, okay?"

This sentence, which she never heard him say then because she stormed away after telling him he was ruining her life, feels prophetic. Actually, he's only asking her to take care of her mother *tonight*. She's upstairs in bed with pneumonia. If she had been well, Cassie and her father would never have gotten into a fight.

She was upset because her father insisted she stay home and watch over mother. If her condition worsened the doctor would need to be called. But Cassie thought her mother was already on the mend, and she was convinced life as she knew it would be over if she didn't get to the party she'd been anticipating for weeks now. She'd only just begun dating Julian and was certain he'd switch his attentions to another girl if she didn't show up.

On this night, she stomped upstairs to her room, slammed the door, threw herself on the bed, and wept for half an hour. Her last actions before her father went to his death. On his way home from the event, a drunk driver traveling in the wrong direction on the freeway smashed into his car. The drunk driver survived but her father did not.

"Don't go, Dad," she says.

He takes out his wool cloak from the front closet. "That's enough, Cassie. You can skip one party and your social life will survive."

She follows him. "I don't mean that. Forget the party. I'm not going anyway. But you need to stay home. Mom needs you. I need you."

He hesitates, surprised by her tone. "I have to go. You can keep an eye on Mom." He kisses her forehead before putting on his coat.

"Please don't go. Please. For me. I'm begging you."

"This is too much. You're being ridiculous." He opens the front door.

"Wait. I have to tell you something. If you go, you'll die in a car accident. I know this for a fact."

"You have a crystal ball? This is over the top even for your imagination." He goes outside.

She considers telling him about the time travel, but knows that won't work either. He's not going to believe it for a minute; he's still thinking her objections are all about the party. She racks her brain for a solution as he pulls the door closed behind him.

I can't let him go. Frantic, she rushes into the kitchen and grabs the knife he uses to carve the turkey at Thanksgiving. There's no other way. Cringing, she lays its edge on her wrist. Outside, the car door bangs shut. He'll be gone in a few seconds. She closes her eyes as she slices into her own skin. Blood spurts out. It's more shocking than painful.

Cassie bursts out of the house and sprints in front of the car, forcing her father to slam on the brakes. Still holding the bloody knife, she raises her wrist to show him the damage. The engine shuts off, the door flies open, her father runs to her side. "What have you done?"

"Come inside. Help me bandage it."

"You need a doctor. Lie down in the back." His voice is thick with equal parts anger and panic. She follows his instructions while he fetches a towel from inside. He wraps it tight around her wrist before getting back in the driver's seat. "I'm taking you to the emergency room."

"Okay, Daddy. I'm sorry." She's his little girl who misbehaved again.

He tries to be stoic, but his anxiety shows in the way he swerves out of the driveway and guns it down the street. It would be tragically ironic if they're killed in a car crash that results from the action she took to save him from getting killed in a car crash.

This thought makes her wonder if it's possible for her to die while she's time traveling. "Dad," she says quietly. She's beginning to feel light-headed from the blood loss.

"What is it?"

"You're the best father in the world. I was incredibly lucky to have you."

Before he can reply, she feels the signs of being drawn back to the future. *No.* She doesn't want to leave him, not without being certain she's saved him. But there's no stopping the pull of her own time.

When she wakes in the morning, she springs up, scaring Gio. Her heart fills with hope as she bounds to her window and looks out to see what might've changed. Her car and bike are in the driveway, exactly where she left them.

With a start, she remembers her wrist. It's normal again, uncut and unbloodied.

"Dad!" she shouts. If she altered history, he might be here now. Maybe she and her parents are still living all together in this house. "Dad!" she cries out again.

Gio is too startled to meow for his breakfast. She races from room to room, but everything is just as it was before she went to bed last night. Still there's a chance. If her father is alive, he will likely be in Florida with her mother. She considers calling, but doesn't know what she'll say if her mother answers. *Remind me, are you down there with Freddie or my resurrected father?*

There is a way she can tell for sure, but she hesitates. Part of her prefers to bask in the uncertainty. Is this what Schrödinger's cat is all about? As long as she doesn't look for proof of his death, he's still alive for her.

When she goes downstairs, she pretends he's in the kitchen with her, and chatters to him while she feeds Gio and makes herself a poached egg on toast. She's sure he would've loved her cat.

But after breakfast, she decides it will only make her sadder the longer she keeps up this pretense. She walks to the cemetery. On her way up the hill, she visualizes her father's section without his headstone. She keeps her eyes averted from his spot until the last possible second.

His grave is right where it's always been. At this point she was sure of it. Still, with her stomach closing in on itself, she kneels at his stone and reads the date of his death in case she might've saved him that night only for him to die of something else in the years since then. But the date is unchanged, and she knows her actions had no effect on the course of their family history.

She presses her forehead against the cool granite. Oddly, she finds comfort in having gotten to relive that night. To have taken back the terrible words she spoke. To have witnessed the love that moved him into action to save her, his only child. Not even scolding her for the craziness and irresponsibility of putting him in that position. She truly could not have had a more wonderful father.

Her leap back in time failed the most basic test. History wasn't changed. *Strike one point from time travel and add one to mental illness.*

She's still not ready to go to a doctor. She vows to keep her thoughts empty before falling asleep from now on. She'll count sheep or fish or something. She doesn't want to visit the past anymore. She doesn't want to relive these painful moments without having the power to change them. The disappointment is too overwhelming, not just because of her failure to save her father. His death isn't the only tragedy she wishes with all her heart that she could change.

Chapter Fourteen

DESPITE THE EMOTIONAL trauma of last night and this morning, she makes it to work on time. She's minding her own business stocking new general fiction books on the shelves when Trish comes over.

"Did you have a good weekend?" She says it like she's hinting she knows something.

There's a lot Cassie could say about her weekend, none of which she wants to share with Trish. "It was nice." She picks up another book and scans for its location.

Trish follows her. "My friend Debbie saw you with Grant Wolcott on his boat Saturday."

"Like I said, my weekend was nice."

"I can't believe you're dating him."

"Why not?"

"No, I mean it's amazing. He's so rich. And good-looking. Everyone wants to go out with him."

"Do you want to go out with him?" Cassie says.

"I'm engaged, in case you've forgotten. Otherwise, yes."

"Well don't get too excited. We're just friends."

The manager calls Trish, who's supposed to be manning the cash register.

"Don't be an idiot," she whispers. "Snag him while you can." She hurries back to her post.

Cassie isn't sure if this information makes her more interested in him or less. She's always been contrary that way. She doesn't usually want the things everyone else wants. On the other hand, she's rather competitive and wouldn't mind being the "winner" when it comes to Grant's affections.

With Trish busy, she has time to think again. The evidence is pointing more and more toward her having a screw loose. Her nighttime adventures seem absolutely real to her, but there isn't any way they could be. No one has ever proven that time travel is even possible. Most likely these delusions are the result of her withdrawal from human society. She sees few people other than co-workers and customers at the bookstore. Her mother and Freddie no more than twice a year. And now Grant. That's about it. Maybe her fragile subconscious can't take the isolation anymore, so it's choosing to relive past events.

She thinks it might be time to talk to a therapist or psychologist. Someone whose job requires them to keep her ramblings confidential. She decides to look them up in the Yellow Pages when she gets home tonight. It would be better to get a recommendation from someone, but she's not comfortable revealing her need for psychological help.

The workday passes quickly, and she goes home to shower and change for her date with Grant. Feeling some anxiety about seeing him again, she considers calling and canceling. Actually she's surprised he's not the one canceling after having found her drawing pictures of Julian. If she were him, she'd be running for the hills at this point.

But she reminds herself she needs to work on her mental

health issues, and human contact is a necessary first step. "Do you agree, Gio?" she says to her cat. He licks his paw. *Sure, talking to the cat is a great way to demonstrate how normal I am.*

Grant arrives in his BMW and approaches the door just as she walks out from the house. He's dressed nicely in slacks and a form-fitting button shirt, no suit or tie thank goodness. She's wearing a blue silk blouse over black leggings, and her long gold earrings. From his look it appears he likes what she's done, but he doesn't comment. She guesses he's starting to understand it's better to keep quiet and avoid making her feel self-conscious.

"Is Giovanni's okay?" he says.

"I love that place." This is true, though she's never been there on a date. The last time she ate at Giovanni's was with her mother and Freddie.

He opens the car door for her like the gentleman he is. She would've been fine getting it for herself, but knows he's been trained this way and she's not about to make a big deal out of it. She's troublesome enough without door-opening debates.

Giovanni's is in Ruford, the seaside town to the east of Brumewich. The waiter leads them to a prime view spot that still manages to be intimate with candles and a red tablecloth. The sun is low on the horizon and soon enough they'll get to watch the sky morph into shades of coral over the water. She's already starting to feel better about the date.

She orders the sole and he gets lasagna. They share a bottle of Chianti after she assures him she's perfectly happy to have red wine with fish. Anyone who grew up drinking Boone's Farm accompanied by Cheetos at high school gatherings is not in any position to dictate the rules of fine dining.

Grant wisely leads the conversation away from anything personal. They talk about art and history and literature and cats. He's playing it safe, because if they speak about their lives growing up in Brumewich, they may enter dangerous territory.

After they've gotten back to his car, he turns to her. "My place for some after-dinner drinks?"

The invitation is tempting. She knows what after-dinner drinks really mean, and part of her wants it. Aside from her recent dreams, it's been a long time since she let a man touch her. But she's still uncertain if it should be this man.

"Sorry, I've had enough to drink," she says. Again, he scores points by not arguing with her literal interpretation of his question. When they reach her house and she says good night, he leans forward and kisses her lips. Though she likes the feeling, she doesn't linger. "Thanks, I had a good time."

"Me too." He doesn't spring out of his car to get the door for her, sensing that would be too much and not at all her style. He does wait until she unlocks her front door and lets herself in, before backing out of her driveway.

Several hours later when she settles into bed, she tries to keep her mind blank to prevent herself from wandering back in time. It seems like it would be particularly unfair to spirit away and visit Julian, after having rejected Grant's overtures. However, trying not to think about Julian only makes her do the opposite. Immediately her brain fills with all sorts of memories she struggles to push away.

Worse, she's already having second thoughts about her plan to swear off time travel. Despite her having renounced it as recently as this morning, the desire to revisit past events fills her. There are mysteries waiting to be unveiled. She may not be ready to face them yet, but neither is she prepared to abandon the possibility of doing so.

What's bothering her most is the uncertainty. Are her time jumps real, and if so, why can't she change history?

Does she enter an alternate universe when she goes back? Or a parallel timeline? None of this really means anything to her; they're just words she's read in science fiction stories. It's all too complicated and given that she earned a D in physics, she has little hope of ever understanding it. She has to accept the power she has without trying to explain it.

However, she needs to know if the information she gathers during time travel is true, as opposed to being imagined inside her head. She comes up with a way to test this using Grant, if she can manage a jump back to the very recent past. Closing her eyes, she concentrates on their dinner this evening, picturing the end of it because she doesn't want to repeat it all again. Rehashing the same topics would bore her to death, nor does she have the appetite to stuff in a second meal.

But she doesn't see the harm in a reprise of that luscious molten chocolate cake she split with him. Soon she's spiraling back in time, where her present consciousness plops into her five-hour-younger self. She's getting better at landing, but still manages to drop her fork—full of a precious bite of the amazing cake—onto the floor.

"Oops."

Grant, ever the man-in-charge, signals for a waitress to clean the mess. It's such a classy place, the waitress even offers to replace their entire dessert free of charge. It takes all Cassie's willpower to refuse this.

Time for her to get to the point. She puts a musing look on her face and says, "Who was the first girl you ever kissed?"

Grant's expression transforms, and not in a good way. He almost looks like he did when he discovered her drawing Julian portraits. "What difference does it make?"

Maybe he's just confused because up till now, they've

been avoiding personal topics. "What's wrong? Is it a big secret?" she says in a teasing tone.

He seems to realize he's overreacted. "Of course not. You wouldn't know her anyway."

Being privileged, he went to boarding school while she attended Brumewich High School in town. "Hey, I hung out with some kids who went to private school," she says. "I know this one girl who had a big crush on you and boasted you were her first kiss."

"Who's that?"

"You first." She scoops up the remains of her cake and savors it.

"Sure. It doesn't matter. Her name was Marcia. Marcia Williams. Her family moved away when she was in the middle of high school."

"Williams. I think I remember her. Brown hair?"

"Blond. We dated for a few months, until the summer. Then she was gone."

"Marcia, huh?" she says thoughtfully. "Sounds like a private school girl." She smiles to let him know she's only kidding. One thing is true, she's never heard of her before.

"So who was the girl with the crush on me?" he says.

"Oh I can't tell you that. What if you prefer her over me?"

He clearly likes this response. It's the first time Cassie has indicated she's pleased about his interest in her.

When they get in the car and Grant asks her if she wants to go back to his place, she surprises herself by agreeing this time. The truth is, she has a kind of superpower right now, an ability to try something out without anyone being the wiser. If they make love during time travel, he won't remember— won't know—that it happened. If nothing sparks between them, she can drop him without bruising his ego. Or if it goes pretty well but she still wants to take her time and not rush into a relationship, she can keep him hanging on in present time.

Grant brightens immediately at her response, confident they'll end up doing the deed tonight. When they arrive at his house, he pours her sherry—the nectar of the rich—and they sip it on the deck watching the moon rise over the water. She's glad she came if only for this.

Later, when he draws her into his arms and kisses her, it feels nice but not electric. Maybe she's not ready; maybe there's not much connection between them. She decides she doesn't want to half-ass this thing, even if it's something he won't remember. She'll remember, and she'd rather wait till they have a greater chance of success.

"I should go," she says, pulling back from him.

"Really?" He tries to kiss her again, but she turns away.

"Sorry, I'm just not ready."

A sore-loser expression flashes across his face, but he quickly masks it. "Sure, I'll take you home." The temperature of his voice has definitely lowered a degree or two. She can't really blame him, but still thinks he should be dealing with this better than he is. This test has not shown him in the best light, though she's not ready to cast him aside yet either.

During the drive home, her consciousness somersaults back to its own time.

Chapter Fifteen

CASSIE ASKED GRANT for the name of the first girl he kissed because it was something she didn't know. This morning, back in real time, she's dying to confirm the answer. If it's the same as what he told her during time travel, then it must be real. It will mean she's truly able to cast her mind backward and relive past events. She can't change history, but she can learn things she didn't know before.

Needing an excuse to drop by and see him, she hits on the idea of bringing one of her paintings to show his mother. After all, he suggested she might be able to convince her posh gallery friends to help Cassie, though no doubt he'll be surprised when she actually takes him up on the offer. *Why not?* God knows she can use all the help she can get. But almost certainly, his mother is not going to show Cassie's work to her snooty acquaintances. The last thing she wants is to give them the impression she's a lousy judge of art.

Still, Cassie's pride motivates her to spend time picking out a painting she hopes won't shame her completely. Eventually she decides to go with a stormy seascape. It's a little cliché, but she feels like she managed to do something special with the water and the clouds.

After she gets back from work, she allows another hour for Grant to commute home from Boston before she drives over to his place. He's clearly surprised she took him at his word and brought a painting for his mother to pimp for her. It amuses her, in fact, to hand it over and watch him try to appear thrilled about it. "Hey, this is great. My mother will love it." He sets it down by the door. "Can you come in?"

"Sorry, I have to get back." As usual, she keeps things vague. "Before I go, though… I know this is silly, but I've got a question for you. Who was the first girl you ever kissed?"

Like it did in the restaurant, his expression darkens. She gets a creepy feeling inside, maybe because this is the second time watching his face transform.

"What difference does it make?" he says like before.

She wants to get this over quickly. "What's wrong? Is it a big secret?"

Again, he gets control of himself though he still doesn't look relaxed. "No, but you wouldn't know her anyway."

"Hey, I hung out with some kids who went to private school. I know this one girl who had a big crush on you and boasted you were her first kiss."

"What's her name?"

"You first."

"Okay. It doesn't matter. She was Marcia. Marcia Willis. Her family moved away when she was midway through high school."

"Willis. I think I remember her. Brown hair?"

"Blond. We dated a few months, until summer. Then she was gone."

"Marcia?" she says. "Sounds like a private school girl."

"So who was the one with the crush on me?" he says.

"Oh I can't tell you that. What if you like her better than me?"

He gets that pleased look again.

As she's leaving, it occurs to her he never asked who her first kiss was. Not last night or now.

She's sure it's because he knows the answer is Julian.

Chapter Sixteen

IT ALL COMES DOWN to Julian. Nothing will ever change until she solves the puzzle of him. And now through some miracle she has the means to do it.

After speaking to Grant, she's convinced the time travel is real. The proof lay in how well his past and present responses matched. It was true they varied a bit, but she believes that's because the situation wasn't identical. Someone could ask her the same question three different times, and depending on her mood, she could phrase the answer in as many different ways. That was how it was for Grant: the same answer, slightly different phrasing.

Except there was the little matter of Marcia's last name— *Williams* vs. *Willis.* It makes Cassie think he made her up. If she invented a name, she'd probably use different variations of it every time the subject arose, because there would be no *real* person to remember. Still, it was strange for him to lie about something so unimportant.

Back home, she takes out a notepad and pencil before settling into the comfortable recliner in the family room. Gio tries to climb onto her lap for some petting but she nudges him aside. Thinking over all she's learned since *the change* began, she makes a list:

The Rules of Time Travel

- Current me goes back in time to occupy younger me.
- I can choose when and where by concentrating on it.
- It only happens when I'm relaxed, nearing sleep.
- The time jump ends when I reach a similarly relaxed state or finish what I set out to do or learn.
- The past plays out as it did unless I do something to change it.
- These changes don't affect my present reality.
- I can witness what truly took place as long as I don't interfere.
- Injuries I receive in the past are gone in the present.
- Unknown: If I die in the past, does it prevent my mind from returning to the present (leaving me brain dead)?

It's important to consider what she hopes to accomplish by witnessing the past. She can't change the course of events no matter how much she may wish it. If she discovers the truth is not what everyone believes, she can't bring back proof, nor can she bear witness in a court of law without a rational way of explaining how she came by the information.

Therefore if she does this, she does it for herself alone. She does it to satisfy her own unrelenting need for the truth. This will have to suffice.

When she's finished going over the list, she sketches a picture at the bottom showing a witch in pointed hat seated on a broomstick. The meteorite brought her the powers she's coveted so long, but instead of flying through the air, she'll fly through time. She's become the witch of her imagining.

Part Three: Warrior

CASSIE (AGE 26)

Chapter Seventeen

YESTERDAY, for the first time since Cassie gained the power to travel through time, she slept through the night without going anywhere. She isn't sure why. She suspects it might be related to her own uncertainty regarding the next step. Maybe *uncertainty* is the wrong word. *Dread* is more accurate.

She needs to be more focused and determined today. This power may only be temporary. Given what didn't happen last night, she might have already lost her ability. But she isn't ready to give up.

This morning she called in sick and told Maggie she expected not to make it in tomorrow either. Assuming she's successful, whatever she sees will take its toll, and she won't be able to waltz into work and act as if everything is normal. Not for some time. Already she's noticing a difference in herself. Lately, she doesn't have much appetite. For breakfast she drank half a glass of orange juice and ate dry toast. Her stomach couldn't take any more. She's also popping aspirin every few hours to relieve the pulsing sensation inside her head that began yesterday.

She resolves not to answer the phone during the day in case it's Grant. She just hopes he doesn't come by the house to check on her. It seems unlikely he'd take time away from work to do that, but to be extra safe, she doesn't even go into her studio to paint. Instead, she stays inside and does sketches of Gio to occupy herself.

Around mid-afternoon, she's in the family room listening to Chopin on the record player and attempting to reread *Wuthering Heights*, when her eyelids begin to droop. Seconds later, the doorbell startles her awake. She doesn't want to speak to anyone now, particularly not Grant, but the music is a sure sign she's at home. Still, she decides not to answer. Hopefully whoever-it-is will quickly give up and leave.

But the ring turns into a series of sharp knocks, followed by a woman's raised voice: "Cassie? It's Helen Wolcott. Are you there?"

Grant's mother? This is surprising. She wonders what the woman could want with her. *Your painting is brilliant, have you got any more?* Ha, Cassie knows it isn't going to be that, but still, her curiosity is too much for her. "Coming!" she calls out, hurrying to the door, pretending to be out of breath when she reaches it. "Sorry, I was upstairs," she says, letting Mrs. Wolcott assume she must've been in the bathroom.

The woman has accompanied her stiff new frosty-haired perm with a white linen suit, of all things, making Cassie wonder how on earth she keeps it clean. "Hello, dear," she says. "May I come in?"

"Um sure, it's kind of a mess though."

Mrs. Wolcott presses past her and glances around. In fact it's neater than usual, but Cassie is assuming the woman's standards are much higher than hers, given that she has trained staff to take care of such things.

"Could you please lower the volume?" Mrs. Wolcott

expresses this as a demand, not a question. Cassie decides to turn the record off rather than guess what level she considers quiet enough.

"Can I get you something to drink?" Cassie says, hoping Mrs. Wolcott doesn't ask for coffee, since she's hoarding the little bit she has left to avoid a trip to the store.

"It's too late for coffee and too early for tea." Following this pronouncement, Mrs. Wolcott walks straight into her living room and across to the sliding glass door looking out toward Inner Harbor. "You have a pretty view here." She glances back at her with a judgmental look, as if questioning the right of someone at her low economic status to be situated right next to the water.

"Would you like to sit down?" Cassie says.

"Goodness no. I've been sitting all morning at my desk."

"All right." Cassie stands awkwardly, thinking it would be rude to sit while Mrs. Wolcott stands, as if she's the Queen of England. Meanwhile the woman stares down her nose at her humble home.

Mrs. Wolcott's eyes stop on a small painting Cassie did of her father. "Yours?" she says.

"I did it when I was thirteen." She doesn't want her to think that's the best she could do right now.

"Interesting portrait. You're not without talent," Mrs. Wolcott says, condemning her with faint praise. "I can recommend a teacher. Harry Feingold in Boston. He's brilliant."

"I doubt I could afford him," Cassie says.

"Perhaps you could allow me to help you with that. If you work hard for two or three years under Harry's tutelage, you might reach a level of accomplishment that would not embarrass a gallery owner to display. I have a particular place in mind."

Until now Cassie hasn't dared consider making a career

out of her art. As condescending as Mrs. Wolcott is, she's offering hope that it might be possible someday. On the other hand, Cassie can't help wondering if Mrs. Wolcott is only encouraging her at Grant's request. She fears this may all be a performance unrelated to her talent or lack thereof.

"Unfortunately," Mrs. Wolcott continues, "if I'm to champion your work in the local art scene, there must be no connection of any sort between us. My reputation for identifying talent would disappear if I began promoting anyone with a close connection to our family."

Cassie almost snorts. It's the opposite of what she thought. Mrs. Wolcott hasn't come here on Grant's behalf, but for her own selfish reasons. She's judged Cassie unworthy of her son.

"Are you saying you can only help me if I stop seeing Grant?" Cassie says.

"I'm glad you understand." But Mrs. Wolcott's bullying has the opposite effect of what she intends and increases Cassie's interest in Grant several fold.

"It's a shame. I could've used your help. But I'd rather keep dating your son."

Mrs. Wolcott's eyes narrow at Cassie. "It won't last. You're a pretty diversion right now. When he's ready to marry, he'll pick his own kind."

"What kind is that? Rich? Socially connected? Arrogant?"

The woman shakes her head. "His kind is determined and ambitious. Highly educated. The type who will break barriers and become a leader in business or politics." Her heels click against the floor as she goes into the hall.

Cassie is trying to think of a powerful comeback, to prove her education at Syracuse was as good as anyone's, but her brain isn't quick enough. Sadly proving Mrs. Wolcott's point.

"Trust me, you won't last long with him," she tells Cassie on her way out. "Why let yourself get hurt?"

Cassie follows her to the front stoop and stands with her arms crossed over her chest, watching the annoying woman drive away in her *car-that's-worth-more-than-I'll-earn-in-ten-years* and thinking what a clever retort she'll have waiting for her if she ever comes back.

But when she turns back to the house, she almost laughs to see the painting she gave to Grant propped up by the side of the door. She brings it inside, musing that Mrs. Wolcott's visit has only made her think better of him. It's a miracle he ended up a decent man after having such a mother.

Dealing with the woman's nonsense has exhausted Cassie. She sits back on the recliner, meaning to take a ten-minute nap. Gio claws his way up the back of the chair though he knows that's strictly forbidden, and settles down to sleep beside her head.

Interestingly, Mrs. Wolcott's visit has increased her motivation to get on with things. To learn the truth and finally close that chapter of her life. Therefore, as she tries to relax, her thoughts focus on the night of the murder. A few minutes later, she drifts away from this time, feeling like she's spinning through darkness.

Chapter Eighteen

CASSIE'S TIME jump sends her back to her own room, just after sunset on the night of the murder. She panics at first, thinking she may be too late, but a glance at the clock shows she has sufficient time to get where she needs to be.

Setting aside the sketchpad that kept her occupied this night, she checks her mother's room to confirm she hasn't returned from the party yet. Cassie needs to leave immediately to be sure not to run into her and avoid questions about where she's going. Drunken Freddie might also want to chat about how much his daughter is dying to be friends with her. She can't afford these delays.

Downstairs, her hands shake as she reaches for the keys, showing how nervous she is already. At least she manages to set out in her mother's car without encountering anyone. Driving to within a quarter mile of Thorne Cove, she turns down a side street to park. She doesn't want to risk Julian recognizing her mother's Datsun along the main road. If he thought she was in the vicinity, he might freak out and cancel his date with Teresa. Cassie can't allow that to happen. For her to witness the truth, events must unfold exactly as they did then.

She walks the rest of the way, diving behind trees twice to avoid the headlights of passing cars, even though Julian and Teresa would likely be approaching from the opposite direction. Fortunately, neither of them has arrived by the time Cassie reaches the cove.

Her apprehension increases as she scans the shore and realizes a beach must be one of the worst possible places to spy on someone. There isn't anywhere to hide that's within listening distance. She'll have to settle on the cottage located just beyond where the sand ends. She's pretty certain the owners had not arrived for the summer yet when the murder occurred; otherwise, it probably wouldn't have happened at all. At least not here.

Sure enough, the cottage is dark and the windows shuttered, clear signs it hasn't been opened yet for the season. She kneels behind tall marsh grass along the far side. A bright half-moon lights the shore tonight, giving her a clear view. She doubts she'll hear anything they say, but it's essential she remain out of sight. If they glimpse her, events will be altered and her coming will be for nothing.

She rubs her hands together, trying to get a grip on herself. Despite the warmth of the night, her arms are trembling. The full weight of what she's come here to do is hitting her now. She is about to watch one human being kill another. She's never seen anyone die of anything before, not even old age or illness. The worst she's witnessed is two people who were already dead: her father, and the grandmother of a friend at a Catholic wake. Not the same thing at all.

Worse, she'll have to refrain from screaming or calling out a warning. She can't allow herself to intervene. Anything she might alter here and now will have no effect on the future, she reminds herself. However, there is one change that will return with her to her own time. She'll know something she could only guess at before. She'll know what happened here on this beach tonight.

Waiting isn't easy. The air has grown still and humid. Her skin is damp, her hands clammy. Already she feels as soiled as the act she's about to witness. Moreover, mosquitos are beginning to find her. She should've thought to spray on repellent before she left the house. When they sting her, she has to repress the urge to slap at them. She can't afford to make a sound now.

Her breath catches at the sight of Teresa walking along the sand from the road. She looks ghostly in a diaphanous white dress that billows around her legs. Her long black hair falls loosely down her back. A beach bag is slung over her shoulder and her feet are bare. It eats into Cassie seeing her like this—how could she have ever hoped to compete? Teresa's hips sway as she crosses the beach to the rocks. No question she's fully aware of the effect she has on men.

Teresa lays down her bag and to Cassie's shock, lifts off her dress, exposing her naked body. She's not even wearing underwear. Then she slowly enters the sea until it reaches her waist and dives under.

Cassie shifts her gaze to the other side, and soon Julian appears. At the sound of Teresa's splashing, he turns toward the water. For one gut-stabbing moment, Cassie wonders if she might have to watch them making love. A powerful urge to run away fills her, until she realizes they couldn't have done that. If they had, there would've been undeniable proof that Julian had been with her tonight.

Teresa swims back toward shore and emerges from the water. She doesn't try to cover her body, nor does she walk into Julian's arms. Instead, she gets a towel from her bag and wraps it around herself, tucking it to hold it in place.

Oddly, Julian is keeping his distance and appears to be averting his eyes from her nakedness. He doesn't act like a man in love. Or even a man in lust.

There's something of defiance in her movements, making Cassie wonder if they've recently fought. Maybe it was about her. She wants to believe he's told Teresa it's over between them because she's come back from school. But then there's no explanation for this meeting.

They continue to stand apart. There's no touching or kissing for Cassie to have to endure, *thank god*. She hears them without being able to make out the words. Julian's voice is harsh. Teresa's is softer but seems dismissive. They speak for several minutes while Cassie strains to listen. She's on edge, afraid of when it's going to happen. But as far as she can see, he has no weapon. He's wearing a t-shirt, shorts, and sandals. There's no place to hide a knife on his person. Maybe he left it nearby.

When they finish talking, Teresa takes out a cigarette from her bag and lights it up. He walks away from her, looking unhappy but not in any sort of murderous rage. Still, this must be when it happens. Maybe he'll get the knife from the truck and return. Cassie braces herself as he reaches the road and she no longer can see him.

Teresa is in no hurry. She leans against the rock nearest her, slowly smoking her cigarette. Looking more than ever like an actress in some film; she clearly has a flair for the dramatic. She gazes at the water, the moon. It's weird, but Cassie almost begins to admire her. She's a woman comfortable with her own sexuality. A creature of the senses. She isn't the sort to worry about her makeup, or manicure, or a rumpled dress.

She trusts in her allure regardless of these considerations. Soaking her hair in the water didn't bother her at all. There's something completely natural and almost feral about her.

Cassie notices the silhouette of Julian returning. At least that's what she thinks at first. But when he draws nearer, she sees it isn't Julian at all.

It's Grant Wolcott.

Her stomach clenches and she fights the impulse to retch. Grant's arrival launches a million questions. *How can this be? Why is he here? What does he have to do with Teresa?*

She hasn't seen him yet, because her face is turned the other way and he's made some effort to be silent. Cassie glimpses the shape of a knife in his hand. It appears he's wrapped a red cloth around its handle to avoid getting his prints on it. She can't doubt his intentions any longer, though she has no explanation.

Teresa notices him when he's within ten feet of her and blows smoke toward his face, looking unconcerned. Cassie thinks she says Grant's name. But it doesn't appear Teresa has seen the knife.

He continues toward her with relentless steps and raises the blade. Her face is confused. It happens so quickly she doesn't have time to react—to scream or back away. But then, the rock is right behind her, leaving her with no place to go.

In a second, he's closed the distance between them and thrust the knife into her heart.

Cassie claps her hand over her mouth, struggling to hold in her own cries. Tears stream down her cheeks. Teresa appears to die immediately; at least she doesn't suffer. Grant lets her body fall to the ground as he draws out the knife. He stares down at her, his face twisted with a shocking combination of malice and triumph.

He looks up like he's suddenly remembered there could

be someone watching him. His gaze sweeps past the cottage and seems to pause on the side where Cassie is hiding. A shiver runs through her.

In her effort to see, she may have raised herself too much above the marsh grass. She lowers her head, though that may be worse, he may have spotted her movement. But he doesn't appear to have noticed anything. His gaze moves on.

Seemingly satisfied, he crosses the sand back to the cove entrance, leaving the scene of the crime. Cassie waits a few minutes longer to be sure he's really gone, before rising and approaching Teresa's body. She's not even sure why she's doing this. It's unlikely she'll find any sort of evidence that wasn't uncovered by the police. She thinks… she thinks it's simply that she needs to pay her respects.

Cassie kneels at her side. From her face alone, she doesn't look like a victim of violent death. Her eyes are closed and she appears to be sleeping.

"I would've saved you if I could," Cassie whispers.

A shell cracks behind her. She whirls around to find Grant racing toward her, the knife gleaming in his hand.

She springs up and tries to run back the way she came. It's like a nightmare where she's struggling to sprint but instead her feet drag like she's moving in slow motion. He's faster and she hears him gaining on her. Her mind spins to come up with a defense but draws a blank. He leaps at her, slamming her body from behind, knocking her down. Her head smashes sideways against the sand. He pins her under his weight, and she braces for the thrust of the knife.

But he must've dropped it so his hands would be free for the tackle. His left one wraps around her neck from behind, while the other grips her right arm.

"What are you doing here?" he says.

"Let me go!" She closes her eyes, visualizing her return to

the future. *Go back, go back,* she tells herself, terrified she won't be able to end this time jump before it's too late.

He bends her arm backward, making her cry out. "Answer me."

"I came to find out if Julian was meeting her here." Inside, she's still screaming, *get out of here. Go back, go back.*

"Jealous?" he says.

"Of course I was. Now let me go!"

"You know I can't do that. Not after what you saw."

"Why did you do it?"

"No one betrays me and gets away with it."

While he talks, she feels underneath her body with her left hand. Maybe she can find something sharp. A rock or a shell. "I didn't know you were seeing her."

"Nobody knew. We were keeping it quiet. But then I found out she had that stinking, lobster-chasing, Portuguese son of a bitch on the side."

"I wanted her dead as much as you. I won't tell anyone."

His hands tighten round her neck. "I always liked you. I don't imagine that's any consolation."

She can't breathe. Her mind claws for her own future with frantic desperation. But she stays right where she is, struggling to break free of his chokehold. He's too strong and he has her from behind. The force of his body restrains her.

Panic fills her. Her lungs feel like they're on fire. Her mind is going blank. Her vision clouds with a thousand pinpricks of light. Like the meteor shower that brought her here.

Chapter Nineteen

CASSIE SUCKS in air and breaks into a coughing fit at the memory of what just happened. She's back in the present. The demon who would've killed her, gone. When she rubs her neck, she finds nothing wrong with it. No pain or bruising. The burning in her lungs has disappeared. There's no remnant of what might've happened seven years ago, but actually didn't.

Instead the scars are emotional and psychological. She'll never forget the sensation of his hands around her neck, crushing her windpipe. The feelings of panic and powerlessness that overwhelmed her. If it weren't for time travel, she would've died.

She's still not certain whether her death in the past would cause her to die here, because she's pretty sure her consciousness traveled back before dying. With her oxygen cut off, she must have passed out, and that could've triggered her return.

She pushes these considerations aside as her thoughts turn to the murder. All this time, she wanted to believe in Julian's innocence, but found it impossible to dismiss the evidence against him—because she'd seen both their cars parked at the cove with her own eyes. His motive had always been unclear, though. Did Teresa anger him by threatening to tell Cassie he'd cheated on her? Or did he harbor a twisted, violent nature she'd never once observed during all their time together? These were the sorts of questions that haunted her for years.

Regarding Grant… incredibly, she never considered him before. Yet now that she knows the truth, it feels as if nothing could've been more obvious. How could she have been so blind? When she called him before talking to the police, he played on her jealousy, telling her he'd seen Julian and Teresa kissing. And just Sunday, in the present, when he saw her drawings, he became stiff and cold. The look in his eyes frightened her, the same look he got when they walked past Teresa's grave. Now she understands. His guilty conscience made him think she'd brought him there on purpose.

It's possible he believes she knows something. Maybe he's dating her for that very reason. To find out if she's a danger to him. To do something about it if so.

A sudden noise makes her start. She glances around at the dark corners of the room, looking for Gio. It could've been the sound of him going out through the cat door.

Grant hides his contempt for the working classes well. It must've come from his mother. She made it clear today she didn't want him dating riffraff like Cassie. Teresa was even lower on the socio-economic scale. After high school, she never even went to junior college. Her mother was a bus driver and her father worked as a custodian. That must've been why Grant wanted to keep their relationship secret. It would've put him on the fast track to losing his inheritance.

To take that risk, he must've been obsessed with her. *Good god.* Cassie has a sudden realization. What a blunder, asking him about his first kiss. It was Teresa. It must've been. Because she's certain his answer was a lie. They could've had an on-again-off-again relationship for years. Between her clumsy questioning and the visit to Teresa's gravesite, he's probably convinced she has doubts about him.

She can only imagine his pathetic horror when the girl he has elevated with his attention chooses the lobsterman's son over him. Grant, a man who has wealth, breeding, the finest education money can buy, and at least one ancestor who crossed the Atlantic on the Mayflower. To be cast aside in favor of someone who plucks giant sea bugs from the ocean for a living. His pride obviously couldn't accept this. Better to kill her before anyone finds out, and make sure the usurper takes the fall for it.

Cassie is still stretched out on the recliner where she fell asleep, but time has passed and the room has grown dark. She checks her watch to find it's nearly nine in the evening. Gio must've meowed for dinner earlier, before giving up to forage for mice instead. She can't blame him.

When she leans forward, pain shoots between her brows and she fumbles for the aspirin bottle beside her chair. At the same moment, a soft knock comes at the front door. She freezes in place, praying whoever is there didn't hear the rattle of the pills.

"Cassie?" Grant says from outside in a low voice, probably meant to be soothing but instead it makes her skin crawl. Immediately she remembers him on top of her, his hands clutching her throat. She knows he's capable of killing her.

I can't face him now. I can't face him ever again.

He shakes the knob. She carefully lowers the aspirin bottle, holding her breath, dreading that she may have forgotten to lock the door. But thankfully it doesn't come open. He tries once more, pushing against it, to no avail.

She doesn't dare move an inch in case he hears her. She'll stay where she is until enough time passes that she's sure he's gone. Meanwhile she struggles to calm herself. He might be suspicious, but he can't be sure she knows anything. He has no reason to want to harm her.

She's still waiting for enough time to pass when another sound brings with it the icy chill of terror. The glass door in the living room is sliding open. She curses herself for forgetting to latch it. *What now?* He'll check the house for her. There's nowhere to hide in this room, and he'll see her if she crosses the hall.

"Cassie? It's me." His footsteps tap against the floor. Sticky sweat gathers at the back of her neck. She doesn't know how she can deal with him now. She literally just watched him murder Teresa Patterson, and witnessed the shadow of his malignant soul in his face. She's likely the only living person who knows what he did.

But she has to say something. If he reaches her before she speaks up, he's going to know there's a problem. She can't have him interrogating her. She needs to convince him everything is fine.

"In here," she forces herself to say. Her voice is tremulous. "You better not come in. I'm probably contagious."

His dark silhouette fills the doorway. Where once he might've been a reassuring presence, now he's the opposite. She wants to crawl into the lining of her chair and disappear.

"I'll take that chance. Are you all right?" He turns on the overhead lamp.

She blinks, feeling completely exposed in the stark light. She must look a wreck. It takes all her strength to keep from screaming as he approaches and places his wrist on her forehead. Her stomach roils and she thinks she might throw up.

"I don't believe you have a fever."

"No. It's my stomach." This is true, thanks to him.

"Why didn't you answer the door?"

"I was napping here. I didn't hear you till just now."

He kneels beside her and looks into her eyes, while she struggles to mask her revulsion.

"Did you go to the doctor?" he says.

"Yes," she lies. "He said there's not much I can do. It's some sort of a bug. I have to let it run its course."

He's quiet for a moment. "Why haven't you been answering your phone?"

"Sorry. It's an effort to get to it, and I just haven't felt like talking. I've been sleeping a lot. The doctor said that would be best."

"You could at least have called me. I've been worried about you."

"I'll be fine. In a few days." *If you leave me alone—forever.*

"Is there anything else?" He rests his hand on her arm. The hand that thrust a knife into Teresa. "Have I done something wrong?"

You've done the worst that one human being can do to another. The accusation nearly spills out of her. She clenches her teeth to hold it in. "Of course not," she somehow manages to say.

The silence falls heavy between them. Finally, when she can take no more and is at the brink of crying out for mercy, he straightens. "Okay then. Call me tomorrow? Just so I know how you're doing."

"Sure. I will."

"Can I get you anything before I go?"

She's afraid her "no" sounds harsh and shrill, but he accepts it. He leaves the room and lets himself out the front door, moving at the same measured pace.

She's struck by the sickening thought that he isn't going to go at all. That he will just make the sounds of the door opening and closing, but he'll remain in her house, spying on her, lying in wait until she falls asleep again.

For this reason, she gets up and crosses the hall to look out at the driveway. Relief washes over her as he gets into his car and drives away.

She locks and bolts the doors, front and back.

Chapter Twenty

AFTER GRANT LEAVES, Cassie feels weaker than ever. She drags her feet to the kitchen to see what there is to eat. Gio is back and meowing so she tends to him first. Only one can of cat food left, and not much kibble either. He wolfs down the contents of his bowl without missing a crumb, before disappearing out the cat door to do his business outside.

It's harder to find something for herself, partly because nothing sounds appetizing. She warms up a can of tomato soup she finds in the back of a cupboard and sprinkles it with parmesan cheese. The orange juice is gone and normally she wouldn't have caffeine this late, but since time no longer seems like a rigid concept anymore, she goes ahead and makes herself coffee.

She eats slowly, trying to process everything that's happened. For seven years she's wondered if Julian really could've committed that crime, and now she finally has the answer. But her feelings are all over the place. She should be comforted by the realization that she didn't have such poor judgment as to fall head over heels with a boy capable of coldblooded murder.

But she's not comforted. Not at all. Because Julian was innocent and she should've lied for him. Should've trusted him and done what he asked of her.

Ironically, the one person she might've turned to in this moment of existential crisis is the actual killer. *Thank god I didn't fall in love with him.* Her instincts were telling her something was wrong. Now she loathes him with all her being.

Part of her, the exhausted part, wants to give up. Move away from this cursed town, as far as she can go. But the other part is filled with rage and wants to act. That part dominates.

Grant got away with murder. A person capable of killing a human being can do so again. *Fuck, he would've done it to me.* Which means she has a responsibility now; she can't simply walk away from this. She was granted a special power—how or why she'll never know—but she must use it to expose him. To make him pay for his crime. To prove Julian's innocence. To ensure Grant never kills again.

She needs to return to the day of the murder. She'll go earlier and track Grant's actions. He must've made some mistakes. There has to be evidence, even if it's disappeared in the seven years since then. She won't give up till she learns something she can use against him.

Finishing her meal, she feels energized again. Maybe it's just the caffeine. Or more likely, adrenaline. What she's about to do frightens her, but it also invigorates her.

Chapter Twenty-One

ON THE MORNING before the murder, Cassie-from-the-future arrives in her kitchen just as her mother is getting off the phone with Mr. Harrington. This time she asks to use the car to drive to Julian's, though that isn't where she plans to go. Her mother agrees before heading outside to weed while the weather is still relatively cool.

Cassie is about to leave when an idea occurs. She goes upstairs to use the phone, so that her mother won't overhear the conversation if she comes back into the kitchen. Before dialing, she grabs a shirt her mother left out on her dresser and covers the receiver with it. She's counting on Grant not having heard her voice for more than a year at this point in time, but to be on the safe side, she plans to disguise it as well as she can.

After the phone rings four times, she gets hopeful that he's gone out, which will make this ruse unnecessary. However, at the fifth ring he picks up.

"Hello?" There's a tinge of annoyance in his tone, making her wonder if she woke him.

"Wolcott?" Talking through the shirt, she keeps her voice low and gruff, hoping he won't even be able to tell if she's a man or a woman. She calls him by his last name because it seems like a guy thing to do.

"Who's this?" Now he's definitely annoyed.

"Teresa is hiding something from you. Meet me at the skating pond now if you want to learn more." The skating pond is a Brumewich landmark, located close to downtown. A grassy area surrounds it, where two people planning to meet could easily spot one another.

"What the hell? Who are you?"

"You'll find out soon enough." She hangs up. Assuming he doesn't dismiss her call as a prank, he should be leaving right away. She's counting on his wanting to learn who knows the secret of his relationship with Teresa. She rushes downstairs and to the car, waving goodbye to her mother on her way.

When she's fairly close to the Wolcott estate, she parks on the opposite side of the road. She's not concerned about Grant possibly seeing her mother's car. He would not have any idea what it looks like.

She waits until the street is clear of traffic before darting to the other side, where she clambers over the stone wall onto their property. The wide lawn in front of the mansion is bordered by a dense thicket of trees on both sides, and she uses their cover to approach the entrance to the guesthouse.

She's encouraged seeing no car parked in the driveway, though it's possible Grant keeps his BMW in the four-car garage attached to the main house. Still, there's a decent chance Grant took the bait. To be sure, she pauses for a moment behind a pine tree and peers through the windows. After a moment or two of not glimpsing anyone inside, she decides she better make her move before he gets impatient waiting for a mysterious stranger at the skating pond and comes back home.

She dashes from her tree to the main door and tries it. *Shit.* These rich folk don't believe in the town mantra of unlocked doors, apparently. She checks all around for a spare key: under the mat, inside a planter, above the door frame. It's not in any of the obvious places, and the unobvious ones will take too long to search.

Ducking back under the cover of trees, she makes her way to the rear of the house. From there she must briefly pass into the open again; she prays no one is watching from the main house. But she's in luck, he's left one of the French doors ajar, probably to catch the cooling breeze coming from the ocean this morning. She slips inside.

Her plan is to search the place. There might be something—a note, a picture, a gift of some sort—that ties him to Teresa. She does a quick scan downstairs, thankful for the lack of clutter. But it seems unlikely he'd leave any secret items on the first-floor level, where visitors might easily stumble upon them.

She heads upstairs and into his bedroom, where the elegant design and stunning water view dazzle her. His furniture is all matching maple in a simple, beautiful Shaker style. He's a monster with excellent taste. As quickly as she can, she checks the drawers in the dresser and bedside tables. The most surprising discovery is how neatly he folds his clothing, including his socks and underwear. His closet is so well-organized—suits and dress shirts perfectly pressed, ties hung in order of color—that she has to wonder if a housekeeper has done all this for him.

The one other bedroom upstairs has been converted into a study. It looks like the office of an Ivy League professor, with a ponderous desk of polished mahogany, and two walls covered by floor to ceiling bookshelves. They're filled with thick leather volumes that might've been printed a century ago. She can't resist sitting for a moment in Grant's padded chair, mulling over his hypocrisy. He plays down his wealth while basking in the spoils of it.

Moving on, she searches the desk, and in the second drawer on the right, she finally finds something that makes her tingle with excitement. A ring box. Inside, there's an engagement ring featuring a brilliant diamond that sparkles beautifully when it catches the light from the window. She takes it out from the box to get a better look, and notices etching inside the platinum band. Holding it closer, she reads, *"G.W. & T.P."*

She needs a moment to absorb this. Grant was going to ask Teresa to marry him. Their relationship had actually gotten that far without anyone guessing. She's beginning to understand the depth of his disappointment now. Not that there is remotely any excuse for him. But he must truly have desired Teresa if he was prepared to raise up a member of the proletariat to his elevated sphere.

As she's putting back the ring box in the drawer, she discovers a receipt that had been hidden underneath it. From this she learns the ring came from Dorn Jewelers in Boston, and its value is even greater than the outrageous amount she imagined.

Suddenly she hears the door come open downstairs. Her shock at discovering a ring distracted her; she should've been listening for the car. Now she's trapped up here.

Noises come from the kitchen, like Grant is taking out dishes or something. She replaces the ring and receipt in the drawer, but when she tries to close it, the wood makes a scraping sound that could be heard beyond this room.

All movement downstairs stops abruptly. Knowing he's

listening causes her leg muscles to tighten, anticipating her need for escape. He's probably figured out the phone call was just to get him away from the house.

She ducks down behind the desk, listening to his footsteps coming up the steps. She doesn't think he can see her from the door, but if he enters the room, he'll quickly spot her.

He goes into the bedroom first. She hears the closet door open and close. Her heartbeat races as she struggles to recall if she left everything in that room the way she found it.

His feet rap the tile when he enters the bathroom from the hallway. Metal shrieks as he rips the shower curtain open. If he's checking the bathtub, he's going to look around the desk too. Though she doesn't believe he'd try to kill her over this, the possibility of his finding her has her shivering in terror. She can't erase the feeling of helplessness that overwhelmed her when he pinned her on the beach.

His footsteps pad along the hall carpet, growing closer. They pause at the entrance to this room.

A sharp rap sounds on the door downstairs. Seconds later Grant thumps down the steps. He may think the person knocking is the same one who called and sent him on the wild goose chase.

She breathes again, and carefully finishes closing the drawer that holds the ring. With luck, his glance into the study will have satisfied him that no one is upstairs.

"Mother," he says after opening the front door.

Her reply is muffled.

Cassie decides she needs to get closer. It's important she hear their conversation. Despite the risk of her movements being overheard, she tiptoes across the Persian carpet and slips behind the office door to listen.

"Is anything wrong?" Mrs. Wolcott says.

"I don't know. Someone's idea of a joke. Do you want some coffee?"

"No, thank you."

Too late for coffee, too early for tea, thinks Cassie.

It sounds like he's making it for himself. "Is Dad okay?"

"This morning he couldn't remember my name. But that isn't what I came here to speak to you about."

"If you're going to try to talk me into asking out Diane Perry again, this isn't the time."

A chair scrapes against the floor. "I don't care if it's Diane or another girl like her. But it can't be Teresa Patterson."

"What are you talking about?" he says.

"I know you're seeing her. Your back patio is quite visible from the house."

Fortunately, she must not have been looking out the right window when Cassie arrived, or she would already be busted.

"It's none of your business, Mother."

"Isn't it? You stand to inherit a fortune. It's the responsibility of both of us to ensure you don't marry a woman who's likely to squander it."

"You don't know anything about her. Just because her family is poor doesn't mean—"

"Has she been to college? Does she have any talent beyond working in a department store?"

"She can't afford college. But she's smart."

"Really? Shall we put that to the test?"

The coffeemaker makes percolating noises. "I think you should leave."

"There's one other matter," she says. "I wasn't going to tell you if I didn't have to. Because it's hurtful. But you leave me no choice."

Cassie pictures the hard look in Grant's eyes.

"This morning I drove past the Reis house," she continues. "I saw Teresa letting herself in like she had the run of the place. Don't you think it's odd they're on such terms she feels comfortable doing that?"

A cupboard is banged shut.

"Now the Reis boy, he would be a good match for her. Quite handsome too."

Something shatters, a cup or a dish.

"I'll leave now," she says. "That's all I wanted to tell you."

And it was a mouthful. Cassie didn't know Teresa had gone inside Julian's house. But it explains why she was lingering nearby. She must've come back out right before Cassie arrived.

The front door opens and closes downstairs. More crashing noises come from the kitchen. He's in a fury, she can tell. *God help me if he finds me in this mood.*

A moment later she hears the phone dial. After a pause, Grant says, "Hey, it's me."

Teresa? She thinks so. If only she could hear her side of the conversation.

"You want to have dinner tonight?... Yes, a real restaurant. I'm sick of hiding. I don't care what my mother thinks." His voice grows strained. "You've been going out with friends a lot lately. Fine. Come here later?" Even Cassie can hear the underlying anger in his tone now. "Forget it then. Call me tomorrow."

Teresa has put him off for tonight. No surprise to Cassie. She already knows Teresa is planning to meet Julian at Thorne Cove.

After he hangs up, an eerie silence follows. Cassie holds her breath, wondering what's brewing inside his head. Petrified he might continue his search of the house.

His feet clack across the hardwood floor. What sounds like a closet door is opened. There's the clanging of metal against metal. Then more footsteps toward the back of the house and out to the patio. The place grows quiet.

This might be her only chance to sneak away. But first she needs to verify he won't see her from wherever he's gone. She steals across the hall and peers out the window.

Grant is hunched beside a stately old oak, swinging a golf club over and over, slamming it into the tree, gashing its poor trunk. She's not certain whether he's picturing Julian or Teresa or alternating between them.

She bounds down the stairs, out the front door, and into the grove of trees. But glancing back at the mansion, she's astonished to see the Reis' Chevy pickup parked in the drive-way. *What on earth is Julian doing here?* This development is completely unexpected. Did Mrs. Wolcott call him to give him a talking-to? Or maybe it isn't Julian at all. It might be Armando delivering lobster for an upcoming party.

Whatever the explanation, it could have relevance, and she needs to find out what it is. Ducking back down to the street, she takes the sidewalk to the main entrance. This time, like a legitimate visitor to the estate, she follows the walkway to the front door and rings the bell. She doesn't expect Grant to come over and disturb them. Not in the state he's in.

Chapter Twenty-Two

WHILE CASSIE WAITS at the grand entrance to the Wolcott mansion, piano music drifts toward her from an open window. Even if there were no lobster truck parked in the driveway, she would know it was Julian playing *Rêverie*. The song, with its ethereal refrain, makes her chest ache inside.

A middle-aged woman who is probably the housekeeper answers her ring. "Can I help you?"

"I'm Cassie Moran. I've come to see Mrs. Wolcott."

"Is she expecting you?"

"Yes," Cassie lies, hoping to expedite this process.

The woman hesitates but apparently decides it isn't worth checking with her employer first. "Follow me." She leads Cassie through a dark hallway that opens into a magnificent ballroom filled with natural light from the enormous windows overlooking the ocean. The room's centerpiece is a grand piano, where Julian plays Debussy's masterpiece with his head bent over the keys and his eyes nearly shut. The way he always plays.

Mrs. Wolcott is seated with a newspaper open in her lap and a pencil in hand, most likely working on the crossword. Beside her, Mr. Wolcott, who has dementia, stares at nothing in particular.

"Cassie Moran is here to see you, Mrs. Wolcott," the woman announces before leaving the room.

Julian stops playing and looks up at her in surprise. Mrs. Wolcott raises her eyes from the paper without showing any great interest in the new arrival.

"I apologize for disturbing you all, but I, um, I need to talk to Julian urgently. His father sent me," Cassie says.

Julian shoots to his feet. "Is he all right?"

"Yes, but can I talk to you privately?"

Mrs. Wolcott waves a bored hand toward the patio. Julian leads Cassie outside through the French doors. She glances in the direction of the guesthouse, wondering if they might see Grant still swinging his golf club, but fortunately the place isn't visible from this location.

"Your father's fine. I just wanted to ask what you're doing here," Cassie says in a low voice.

"What are *you* doing here? I thought you were coming over this morning."

"Sorry, I've been busy. I was planning to come by this afternoon."

"I missed you, Cass." It surprises her to hear the rebuke in his tone. She'd almost forgotten they haven't seen each other in six months at this point.

"I missed you too. But right now, I'm wondering why you're here. Do they pay you for this?"

"In a way. Four or five months ago, she found me an incredible new teacher in Boston. When I said I couldn't afford her, she said she'd cover it if I would just come by the house now and then to play for Mr. Wolcott."

"He likes your music?"

Julian shrugs. "He never shows any sign of it. But she says he used to love classical piano. Maybe he's still enjoying it even if he can't say so."

"Does Grant ever come here and listen to you play?"

Julian makes a face. "Grant? One time he walked in and left immediately. I don't think he likes me much."

All she can think is that was nothing compared to how much Grant must loathe him now.

"I'll make an excuse and leave with you," Julian says.

"No." Again she sees the hurt wash over his face. "I'm sorry, but I promised my mother I'd pick up some things at the grocery for her. I'll come by your house later."

He swallows his disappointment and kisses her lightly on the cheek. Inside, he returns to the piano and starts from the beginning. Cassie wishes she could stay and listen. The grand piano highlights Julian's talent in a way his little upright can never approach.

"Please remind your mother I need to receive her clothing donation by this evening," Mrs. Wolcott tells Cassie on her way out.

After reaching her car, she breathes in deeply a few times to settle herself. As difficult as this has been, she's glad she forced herself to search Grant's place. She's gained important information. She knows for certain he will lie to her tomorrow, when she calls him before she's questioned by Officer Brooks. He will tell her he saw Julian and Teresa making out at the cove two weeks earlier. But clearly, judging from his attack on the tree, Grant first heard about their relationship today from his mother.

Secondly, Cassie discovered the ring and she knows where it came from. If the store has kept records for seven years... well, it's too soon to get hopeful about that. She's not sure how useful it will be. Buying someone an engagement ring is no proof of murder.

Lastly, she has to wonder if Mrs. Wolcott, following the murder, will come to suspect her own son. Because she's the only one who knows he has a motive.

Chapter Twenty-Three

CASSIE HAS one remaining task to perform before the killing takes place tonight.

She drives across town and over the railroad tracks to where Teresa Patterson lives on the right side of a tired duplex. Cassie spots her seated on the sidewalk in front of her home, playing jacks with a boy of eight or nine. The resemblance between them reminds her that Teresa had a little brother. *Beloved Sister* it says on her headstone. The thought pinches Cassie's heart.

Continuing past them, she turns the car around at the next intersection and returns to park several houses down from the duplex. She remains in the car, watching the siblings play. They're so intent on their game, and so completely at ease with one another, neither one notices her. Now and then, Teresa ruffles his hair or kisses his cheek. They laugh a lot, particularly when she pretends to try to get away with cheating. It appears she helps him to win at the end.

What Cassie sees moves her. She's never even considered who Teresa was as a person, aside from being the girl who stole Julian's heart. Until now, she never wondered about her talents and skills, her hopes and dreams, or her friends and family members. Most likely they'll grieve for the rest of their lives, especially this brother of hers. Just like Cassie will never stop feeling the pain of her father's loss.

Before long they gather the jacks and climb into Teresa's car. She's working at Filene's this afternoon—Cassie knows this—and must be planning to drop off her brother at their parents' house on the way. Cassie keeps her face lowered as Teresa checks her rearview mirror, backing out of the driveway.

After the car turns the corner up ahead, Cassie goes to the door and tries the knob, though it doesn't surprise her to find it locked, given that Teresa lives alone. She checks all around for a spare key, and this time she gets lucky and finds it under a conspicuous rock near the steps. Glancing around to make sure no one's watching, she lets herself in.

It's a small place, just a sitting room, table area, tiny kitchen and a half-bath downstairs, two cramped bedrooms and a closet-sized bathroom upstairs. It seems clean enough, but messy. A couple jackets and a blanket on the couch. Some wrappers and an empty beer can on the coffee table. Dishes in the sink and so on. She does a quick check downstairs, not expecting much. If Teresa was dating two guys they might drop in sometime and she wouldn't want them seeing photos of each other.

The main thing she learns in the sitting room is something she never would've guessed about her. Teresa likes to knit. On a side table, she's left out a pink mohair sweater in progress. And inside the front closet, there are hats and scarves of various styles, colors, and types of yarn. She has a flair for this. Unlike Cassie, who's always been terrible at knitting because her attention wanders and she lose stitches.

Continuing upstairs, she glances in the medicine cabinet, not surprised to find a packet of birth control pills. Sensible girl to be doing her best to avoid pregnancy at a time when she might be unable to name which man was the father.

She moves on to the spare bedroom, which holds a spindly chair, a rickety desk, and a bookshelf filled with fashion magazines. It occurs to her this "study" is the exact opposite of Grant's. In some ways she agrees with Mrs. Wolcott: they seem like such a mismatched couple, it's inevitable things wouldn't work out between them. If only Grant could've accepted that.

She riffles through the drawers but they're mostly empty save for the usual stuff like pens, paper, a stapler, and scissors.

Finally she's in Teresa's bedroom where she hopes to find something, anything, that ties her to Grant. Maybe he gave her a piece of expensive jewelry, but the police had bigger clues so they never traced it. This could be more important than the engagement ring, which he probably returned to the store, where they would've removed the engraving that provided evidence it may have been intended for Teresa. That would still be an assumption based on initials alone. But if he'd given her something else, and if her brother now had it, maybe it could be traced to the same place where he bought the ring. If they had a receipt showing his name, this would establish their connection.

A search of her one bedside drawer turns up a few loose photos of her and her little brother. One of her parents, or at least Cassie assumes that's them. No pictures of Grant or Julian. Moving on to the dresser, she finds a large jewelry box in Teresa's top drawer and sorts through its contents. She's no expert, but it all looks like costume jewelry to her. Nothing one couldn't find in a J.C. Penney catalogue. Not the sort of thing Grant would buy for her, or if he did, it wasn't special enough to be traced back to him.

She does a quick sweep of the rest of the dresser, starting to feel like this visit has been a complete waste of time. However, at the very back of the bottom drawer, her fingers poke a small box. She snatches it out with a surge of excitement, thinking *this is it, this is what I've been waiting for.*

A necklace is folded inside: a smooth silver disc on a silver chain. The shape of a heart is etched on the disc, along with the words, "Adoro-te."

The adrenalin drains from her and she has to sit down. When she squeezes the necklace inside her fist, it feels like it's burning into her flesh. She flings it across the room.

The language is Portuguese. Julian has said those words to her before. But he never gave her jewelry inscribed with it.

She wishes with all her soul she'd never come here.

Chapter Twenty-Four

WHEN CASSIE WAKES in her own time, it's mid-morning and poor Gio is beside himself with hunger. She feels like a terrible cat-mother.

She empties out the last of the kibble in Gio's bowl. It's a meager amount. As for her own meal, the fridge is mostly empty and the cupboards are nearly bare. She can't avoid a trip to the grocery store any longer.

In the middle of getting dressed, she hears the phone ring and decides she better answer it to avoid more visits from anyone checking up on her. It's Maggie, her boss from work. Cassie makes her voice thick and hopes she sounds deathly ill, even though she considers it unlikely she'll still have a job at the end of this. She refuses to let herself worry about it; there's too much else at stake right now. And it isn't a lie that she's feeling ill. Her head aches, her face is wan. If she doesn't finish this soon, it may finish her.

After hanging up, she pops two more aspirin and heads out to the car. The phone rings again inside the house, but she doesn't have the energy to run back and answer it.

Whoever is calling, let them assume she's busy throwing up in the bathroom.

She drives to the least popular market in town, hoping not to see anyone she knows. Once inside the store, she races through the aisles, putting little thought into what she's buying, just trying to finish quickly. She fills her cart with cat food, eggs, bread, dairy, fruits, and veggies. There's a line at the register, but no one appears to recognize her. She breathes a little sigh of relief once she's back in her car.

At home, she takes two bags from her trunk, leaving the kibble and one more bag for a second trip. With both arms full, she reaches out her hand to insert the key into the knob. This is when she discovers the door isn't locked.

She hesitates. Didn't she lock it on her way out? She's pretty certain she didn't bother with the bolt, which would've required the key. But locking the knob only meant turning it on the inside before shutting the door after her. She thinks she did that.

On the other hand, it's true she forgets to lock up now and then. Her mother used to scold her for it sometimes. This is probably one of these occasions.

Kicking the door inward, she steps inside and sweeps the house with her gaze. Everything appears just as she left it. If someone had broken in, they probably wouldn't worry about making a mess. She waits a moment longer just listening, but the place is quiet.

Continuing into the kitchen with the bags, she begins to unpack them. But seeing the canned cat food reminds her Gio ought to be under foot right now. He usually greets her when she arrives, especially when she's carrying anything. Always hopeful of a meal.

She uses the electric opener on the chicken with gravy. Normally, its sound has the same effect on Gio as the buzz of an oven timer on a human being, drawing him instantly to the kitchen. But this time, he still hasn't appeared after the can snaps open.

She fills his dish and sets it on the floor before going to the hall to listen again. Nothing at first. Then a muffled meow.

"Gio?" she calls out.

He meows again but still doesn't come. She follows his faint cries to the family room, and from there, to a closet where games are kept. When she opens the door, he leaps out from a shelf but doesn't race off to his food. Instead, he stays close like he wants her protection.

How did he get shut in here? She bends to pet him while looking back at the doorway, feeling a tingle at the back of her neck. Someone did this to him. Someone who wanted him out from under foot.

A floorboard groans somewhere in the house, causing the tingle to race down her spine. At the same time, an idea flashes into her head. Turning back to the closet, she gets out her father's favorite baseball bat, a 1962 Louisville Slugger.

She returns to the hall with silent steps. The front door is still ajar as she left it when she came in with the bags. Could the intruder have run off? She glances out the opening without seeing anyone.

Gio slips past her feet and goes to the kitchen now, unable to resist the scent of his food any longer. Continuing from room to room, Cassie checks all around until only the second floor remains. She hesitates at the bottom of the steps, frightened at the thought of being trapped up there by the intruder. Maybe she should call the police, except she's not sure she wants them coming here, asking questions. There are too many inexplicable aspects to her life at the moment.

She steels herself and goes up the steps, glancing quickly into each room, holding the bat ready to swing. Seeing no one, she does a more detailed search. Inside the closets, behind the shower curtain. No one.

She returns to her own room for a more careful examination. The second drawer in her dresser is crooked and not quite closed. This happens when one doesn't know the trick of holding it with both hands and lifting up on the left. For Cassie, it's just instinct to close it the right way, because she's done it so many times.

She notices other small changes. A sketchpad turned down when she believes she left it face up. In the closet, her Julian box is not quite in its place. Dragging it out, she checks inside but nothing appears to be missing. This was no thief, though. A thief would not be so neat. A thief would steal anything they could pawn, even things of small value, like the earrings and silver ring Julian gave her. As far as she can tell, nothing has been taken from the house.

One more thing occurs to her and sends her rushing back down the stairs into the family room. She has left her list of time travel rules in a drawer. It's still there, and doesn't appear to have been moved. But she can't be certain. Likely if he saw it, he'd consider it the ravings of a lunatic. Maybe that would be all right. He might underestimate her.

This must have been Grant. Maybe he was the one who called as she was leaving for the store, trying to confirm whether she was home. As far as she knows, no one else has a motive to search her house. He wants to know if she has any sort of evidence that could be used against him. It's unlikely after all these years. He must believe if she had solid proof, she'd have brought it to the police long ago. But clearly the possibility is eating away at him. He might've hoped she kept a journal where she had written down her thoughts. *Ha*, the only thing in writing is the insane time travel list.

He may not have had a chance to search anywhere other

than her bedroom. Most likely her arrival interrupted him. It gives her a chill thinking he must have crept down the stairs and slipped outside while she was getting Gio out of the closet. Thank god he didn't hurt her cat.

She fetches the remaining groceries from her car, and bolts her door when she's back inside. At least Grant ought to stay away for the rest of the day now. This makes everything all the more urgent. With him becoming more reckless, she needs to finish her fact-gathering as quickly as possible.

Though it broke her heart to find that necklace from Julian in Teresa's bedroom, she's aware her hurt feelings are insignificant compared to the much larger issue of exposing Grant as the killer. For this reason, she returns to her bed immediately following a quick lunch.

However, she lies on the sheets so ridiculously awake, her eyes won't even stay closed. No matter how hard she envisions the time where she wants to land, nothing happens. It appears she'll be forced to wait till night to continue.

Just as she gets up, though, she remembers something that may be useful. She still hasn't packed away the things her mother left behind, though she's been meaning to do it for months. Her mother used to take the occasional sleeping pill until Freddie talked her into giving them up. Cassie is pretty sure she noticed a bottle in her bathroom not long ago. Checking it, she finds a few tablets remaining. With luck, she won't need more than this.

Chapter Twenty-Five

IT'S dinnertime on the day of the murder. Cassie is in mid-bite landing in her nineteen-year-old self. Right away she feels the difference. This young body of hers has a strength and energy the older one is currently lacking.

The sounds of her mother getting ready for her big date come from upstairs.

She finishes her meal, since this version of her seems to be hungry, before going upstairs to change into her spying clothes. Simple dark t-shirt and jeans. Ankle socks, black sneakers. They're the quietest shoes she has.

At this point, her mother shouts to her from the kitchen, asking if she'll bring the box of used clothing to the Wolcott's house. Cassie yells back, *sure*, even though she has no intention of going there this time. They exchange shouted good-byes when Freddie arrives. Thankfully the two leave quickly.

Cassie thinks about bringing her polaroid camera tonight. How amazing it would be to unearth incriminating photos in the future. But she's well aware her actions here don't change anything, nor can she carry photos with her when her consciousness swoops back to her present-day self. These limitations make her job a thousand times harder.

After the lovebirds have driven away, she returns downstairs and gets herself a cup of coffee. She must be as alert as possible tonight. When the sun finally lowers, she leaves on her bike. She's not sure when Julian will be setting out from his house, but she needs the cover of darkness to be sure no one notices her. It's past nine when she reaches the next street over from his, where she ditches her bike behind a play structure in someone's yard.

Approaching Julian's place, she's glad to see the truck gone. She knows now he probably did meet his friends before going to the cove. At the time she thought he hoped they would provide his alibi. Now she thinks he simply wanted some part of his excuse for not seeing her tonight to be true.

Light glows from the front windows. She peeks through the glass and sees Armando seated in the corner chair next to the lamp. His head is bent over a bound notebook in his lap, with his hand poised above it holding a pencil. After a pause, he writes something on the page.

She's filled with curiosity. Did Armando keep a journal? She never saw evidence of it before, but then, as a teenager, she barely noticed him. He was a parent, after all, even if a young one. Who ever paid attention to what their friends' parents were doing?

She has to wait for him to finish and leave the room. Hopefully, no one will pass in the street and notice her lurking outside the Reis house. To be sure, she slips around the side, avoiding the windows, and ducks down behind the trash can. It doesn't take long before the light in the main room is shut off, and a different light comes on in Armando's bedroom window at the back.

Soon that too is extinguished. She waits another ten

minutes or so for good measure, to be sure he's fallen asleep, before returning to the front and letting herself in. She had been planning to go directly upstairs, but it occurs to her Armando's journal might possibly hold some clue to Julian's behavior. At first it appears he took it to bed with him, until she checks the drawer in the table beside the chair and discovers it tucked inside there.

Cassie brings it to the window to read it under the light from the street. But when she flips to the first page, she finds he has written in Portuguese. *Duh.* She wants to kick herself for not thinking of that. His English is fine but he would naturally feel more comfortable writing in his native tongue.

However, before closing the book, she notices how the words seem to be written in stanzas. It's poetry, she realizes with a shock. Skipping ahead to scan more pages, she discovers a series of what appear to be poems identified by neat titles at the top.

She smiles to herself. All this time she thought he did nothing but catch lobster by day and watch TV by night, and here he was writing poetry. He must have the soul of a romantic and she'd had no idea. So much for her powers of observation.

Toward the end of the book, a title strikes her eye: *Para Teresa.* She knows enough to guess it means "For Teresa."

Confusion fills her. Why would Armando be writing poetry for Teresa? Could it be some other Teresa? Or maybe he wrote this for Julian to use, helping his romantic pursuits like a fatherly Cyrano de Bergerac. If that were the case, though, why had Cassie never received a poem from Julian? Other than a purposely inept one he gave her on Valentine's Day one year, beginning with the ridiculous "Roses are red, Violets are blue" and going downhill from there.

The sound of a snore from the back room breaks her

reverie. She has things she has to do, and since Armando is apparently asleep, she must get to them. After quietly restoring the book to its place, she slips upstairs, avoiding the steps that groan under a person's weight, amazed she remembers which ones they are. It surprises her to find Julian's door shut because he usually leaves it open. She wonders if he might be home, but then who could've taken the truck?

The room is empty as expected, though. She turns on his lamp so she can look around, and immediately notices a folded note on the bed. The paper looks like it's been crumpled, reminding her of Julian's confusion when she arrived at his house this morning. The way his fist tightened around something, and how he shoved it in his pocket like he didn't want her seeing it. She opens the note now and reads: "Meet me at Thorne Cove at 11. Teresa."

She swallows hard. Here it is, the reason Teresa came to the house. She must've dropped off the note before Julian got back. That and the stupid heart-shaped cookie Armando claimed for himself to save his son from discovery.

She hears noises downstairs, like someone's coming in. It could be Julian—or another person. The stairs creak loudly. Whoever it is doesn't know which steps to avoid. With no time to lose, she flies into the closet and closes the door except for a crack she can spy out of.

Julian's door opens slowly. She only has a limited field of vision, but as the man enters the room, she glimpses enough of him to tell it's Grant. This is what she expected, but still her heart beats wildly. She hears paper crinkling as he picks up the note. After he reads it, his hand closes over it, squeezing tight like he wants to make it disintegrate. He blows out a sharp breath before leaving the room and returning down the stairs.

She waits a few moments longer before coming out. The

first thing she notices is that the note is gone. He didn't throw it in Julian's wastebasket, so he must've taken it with him.

Tiptoeing to the hall, she looks down the steps. Grant is just leaving, pulling the front door shut behind him. She crosses to the storage room upstairs and keeps herself hidden as she peers out from the side of the window. Grant has paused near the entrance as he inserts a long knife into his backpack. He draws on the pack while rushing to the side of the house. She can't see what he's doing there. He returns shortly, grabs the bike he left near the truck, and pedals away.

Recalling Armando telling her the murder weapon came from their kitchen, she hurries downstairs to check the butcher block that holds their cutting and carving knives. Sure enough, there's an empty slot that looks like it held the largest of them. Here is proof that Grant has already made up his mind to kill her and frame Julian. Proof that he's acting with cold deliberation, perhaps from the moment he read the note and knew where he would find them together. Later, he'll be sure to leave the knife where it will be found. When they search the Reis house, police will easily match it with the set. When that happens, Julian will lose all hope of proving his own innocence.

She goes out the front door and around to the side, wondering what Grant was doing there. Opening the lid of the garbage can, she discovers the crumpled note where he placed it inside. Tomorrow when the police come with their warrant, they'll find it and might wonder how any killer could be stupid enough to cover his tracks so poorly. But with all evidence pointing to Julian—including Cassie's eyewitness account that places him at the cove at precisely the right time —they'll still be convinced of his guilt.

Filled with an impotent rage, Cassie leans against the clapboard, pressing her hands hard against it. Teresa's killing is the greatest horror, but the calm way in which Grant has set this trap for Julian is nearly as monstrous. He'll destroy two lives without flinching.

Before long, she recognizes the noise of Julian's truck as it approaches from the street and swerves into the driveway. Its door comes open and is slammed shut. A bang follows Julian's entrance into the house. She resists the urge to go to him, warn him, tell him everything she knows. Because it won't change anything.

Gazing up at the light from his bedroom window, she wonders if he's noticed the note is gone. If so, he probably doesn't think much of it. He may believe his father found it and threw it away. A moment later, his light goes out. Julian has no idea regarding the tsunami that will overwhelm him tomorrow. Probably he'll even sleep soundly tonight, despite his apparent irritation with Teresa.

One thought continues to nag at her. Armando's poetry. *Para Teresa.* Why would he write such a thing? A new idea is taking hold inside her. She might never get another chance to find out if it's true. Despite the resolution she made only minutes earlier, not to disturb Julian, she returns to the front of his house and enters again. She glides up the stairs to his door, where she knocks lightly and whispers his name.

Seconds later the door is flung wide. He gathers her in his arms. "How'd you know I was dying for you to come?"

He tries to kiss her but she resists and makes him sit beside her on the bed. She says what she should have said to him seven years ago. "I know you went to see Teresa at Thorne Cove. I saw your truck."

"And you thought…?" He slips one arm around her waist. "You couldn't think… Cass, I wasn't cheating on you. I never have."

"She has a necklace. It says 'Adoro-te.'"

"Does she? That doesn't surprise me."

"She left a note for you to meet her." All the accusations, gushing out of her.

He glances around for it. "Were you here earlier? I left it on my bed."

"It upset me to see it. I threw it away." It won't help to tell him anything about Grant.

"But it wasn't for me. She left it for my father," he says.

His father. *Para Armando.* Then perhaps it's true, Cassie thinks. Like his son, the man had an undeniable appeal to women. The same shiny black hair and muscular physique. He had a roguish charm and appeared younger than his age. His devotion to Julian was evidence of a warm heart.

"I found it in his room this morning. I took it away without telling him," Julian says.

"Why would you do that?" This part makes no sense.

"He's been quietly dating her since before Christmas. But last week, I saw her with Grant. Figured she would dump my father. I didn't want him getting hurt."

"Don't lie to me." She's lived with a different belief for so long, it's a struggle to wrap her head around this new information. But then she remembers what she saw the night of the murder. His eyes averted from Teresa's naked body. He never touched her. He kept his distance.

"I swear it's true. I went there to tell her to leave him alone," Julian continues. "To ask her to find an excuse to let him off easy. But she said she was breaking up with Grant. She loves my father. Can you believe it?"

"I can, actually." Teresa probably had begun to sense the corruption inside Grant. As Cassie has.

"You wanna know something? I've been an ass. I didn't just go there for my dad's sake. I wanted her to break it off with him for my own selfish reasons. You know why? Mrs.

Wolcott. If Grant finds out he got dumped for a Reis, I can kiss my piano lessons goodbye. And she promised to help me get into the conservatory. But he's gonna be so pissed, he probably won't rest till he gets her to totally sink my chances of a career."

Oh he's going to do so much worse than that. Cassie lays her head against his shoulder.

"Screw them," he says. "I want my father to be happy."

"Why didn't you tell me before?"

"It was his secret. Him and Teresa. You know? Didn't think it was mine to share."

"It would've made all the difference." Her heart is shattering. If she'd known, she would've told a thousand lies for him. But instead she was petty and jealous and suspicious.

"I would never cheat on you," he says.

"It was Armando all along?"

"I swear it."

She closes her eyes, drowning in regret. A fire starts inside her head and takes her away.

Chapter Twenty-Six

IT'S early evening when Cassie returns to the future. Her first thoughts: *Julian never cheated. Armando was in love with Teresa.* She pushes them back, refuses to let herself think about them. Otherwise, the revelation will overwhelm her and she'll never complete what she set out to do.

She feels a weird combination of exhausted and sleepless. It's essential she finish this thing soon. Just one more trip, she thinks. One more trip to allow the final chapter to play out.

After making herself an omelet, she sits in the kitchen to eat and consider her next move. So far, despite what she's observed of Grant's actions, she doesn't know how to prove he's the killer. She can only imagine Officer Brooks' reaction if she skips into the station, reveals everything she knows, and tells him she discovered it all through time travel. Oh, that would go over well. Especially since there's such an obvious rational explanation for how she knows details that were never publicly revealed. *She knows because she's the killer herself,* they would say. Murder by reason of insanity would no doubt be the verdict.

But she's come this far, she refuses to give up now. There's more to learn on the day following the killing. Maybe she'll find out Grant made a mistake she can somehow use against him. She has to try.

Every second she delays brings her closer to the time when Grant will come back to her house to check on her. She can't bear to look at him right now. She needs to get through all of it, and then she'll sit back and figure out a plan. If a plan is even possible.

The unpleasant smell of an old sock hovers in the kitchen, and it isn't her omelet. *It's me*, she thinks after sniffing around. She hurries upstairs to the shower, a place she hasn't visited in several days, and peels off her clothes. Her hair is greasy and her skin sticky. But when the warm water pours over her, no matter how hard she scrubs, she can't remove the feeling of violation that's enveloped her.

Putting on a clean outfit makes her feel a little better. She goes outside and collects the newspapers that have gathered, plus the mail that's overflowing from the mailbox. She would've done that when she returned from the supermarket, but the signs of an intruder distracted her. She glances through the bills and decides she has a few days to take care of them. Lastly, she rechecks that all the doors and windows are secured. It's possible Grant has already learned how to pick locks, but at least she has to do what she can to try to keep him out.

She's ready now. To guarantee she'll be able to sleep, she takes another of her mother's pills. Closing her eyes, she concentrates on the day following the killing, shortly after Officer Brooks' departure.

When she lands, she's in her bedroom weeping. She stifles a sob and goes to the bathroom to blow her nose and clean her face. Nothing she can do about her swollen eyes.

Checking the time, she hopes she hasn't cut things too close.

She tries not to think too hard about her next step, or she might lose her resolve. It's essential for her to observe what Grant is doing in the aftermath of the killing. Most likely he's spending the day covering his tracks in every way possible. She can't do anything with destroyed evidence, now or in the future, but knowing what he's done, understanding what he believes to be incriminating, still might help her when it comes to formulating a plan.

When Cassie comes downstairs from her room, she finds her mother in the kitchen preparing to fry up some chicken.

"I have to go out," she says. "I'll need the car."

"Have you seen the weather?"

She looks out the window, where wind-driven rain beats against the glass. "I'm not going far. I'll drive carefully."

Her mother breathes out heavily. "Honey, you know you can't go see him. You have to stay out of this."

"I'm not going there. I'm going to see Shawna." She was Cassie's best friend in high school. "I really need to talk to a friend right now."

"At least eat some dinner first."

"I have to go right away. The weather is only supposed to get worse."

Her mother sighs again. "Fine. Drive carefully. Don't slam on the brakes. During the last nor-easter, Mrs. Lindley slid all the way down—"

"I know, Mom." Cassie takes the keys, grabs her rain jacket, and hurries out before the permission is withdrawn. She would've gone with or without her mother's consent, but it feels better this way.

Outside the storm is as bad as she remembers, and the sky is growing dark. At least not many drivers are stupid enough to be on the road. Her windshield wipers are swiping back and forth at full speed, but it's still difficult to see anything. She turns a corner and confronts a thick branch on her side of the road. No choice, she has to brake hard, and her car swerves left. A jeep coming the opposite way screeches to a halt barely in time to avoid hitting her.

She backs up, and after the other car passes, manages to get around the branch on that side.

Down the street from the Wolcott estate, she parks at the curb and hurries up to the house, splashing through puddles in her sneakers, wishing she'd remembered to put on boots. Like before, she sneaks among the trees till she's close to the guesthouse.

What she sees upon approaching shocks her. Julian is here, rattling the doorknob and shoving against the door. When he can't get in, he doesn't do the sensible thing and check around back. Instead he hurls a rock through one of the glass panes. Once it shatters, he covers his hand with his sleeve and reaches through to turn the knob inside. He leaves the door ajar behind him when he goes in. Shutting it doesn't matter when it's obvious there's an intruder inside.

So Julian knows… or suspects. Another piece of information Cassie never had. This new knowledge forces a change in her plans. The question is, should she reveal herself to him? Her mind says it isn't a good idea, but her heart drives her forward into the house.

He's already upstairs. The sound of drawers being yanked out and thrown on the floor come from the bedroom. He's frantic, searching for evidence against Grant. She races up the steps to join him.

"Julian, it's me," she says before entering, in case he thinks she's Grant and is preparing to bash her over the head with something.

He looks up from the mess of Grant's possessions he's made on the floor. "Cass?"

"Julian, I'm so sorry. I couldn't lie for you."

He doesn't look surprised. "It's all right. I shouldn't have asked you."

"I'll help you search."

"You believe in me? Even after—"

"I know you didn't do it."

"Grant was seeing Teresa," he says.

She resists saying *I know* again.

Julian freezes at the sound of a car outside. "Fuck. He's back. Don't let him see you."

"What are you going to do?"

He doesn't answer, just hurries past her to the stairs. She debates following him, but there's one other thing she wants to check. Going into the study, she searches his desk again for the ring, without finding it this time. She scans the room for another hiding place, and discovers Grant has a safe. Probably it's in there. Maybe it's still in there, seven years later.

"What the hell are you doing in my house?" Grant says downstairs.

There's a loud bang, like someone got slammed up against the wall. She thinks it must be Grant.

"You killed her, you bastard," Julian says.

Grant sounds like he's gagging. "You're crazy. I barely knew her."

"Don't lie to me! I saw you together."

"You're the one lying."

"She humiliated you. Richest family in town and she chose a guy who's got nothing."

A bang like someone's head hitting the wall. "You're gonna confess," Julian says. "You're gonna call the cops right now and tell them you did it."

"Or what?"

"Or I'll kill you," Julian says.

The table bangs and scrapes against the floor. It sounds like Grant escaped Julian's grip. She hears fists hitting flesh and bone. If Grant were not still alive in the future, she would seriously wonder if Julian is about to beat him to death.

"Stop it!" Mrs. Wolcott calls out. Cassie wonders if she heard the commotion from her house. More likely she's been keeping a close eye on her son.

The noises stop. Julian is not really capable of killing anyone, especially with Grant's mother watching.

"Leave my son alone," she says.

"He did it," Julian says. "He killed her."

"My son would never do such a thing. He was home with me. We played cards in the main house. His father sat with us."

One of Cassie's most important questions now has its answer. How far would Grant's mother go to protect him? *All the fucking way.*

An alibi from one's parents shouldn't count for much, just as Julian once said. But this is Mrs. Wolcott. The most influential woman in town. And the toughest. No one likes to cross her. Whatever she wants, she only need make a generous donation.

"The police are on their way," she says.

"You're lying about Grant. He wasn't here." Julian's voice drips with resignation. He knows this visit was ill-considered. But he couldn't help himself.

"Why don't you let the police sort it out?" she says.

It sounds like Julian leaves the house. Cassie looks out the front window and sees him paused outside, staring up at her. There's no point in his waiting. She waves him on, trying to show she'll be all right. He must realize there's nothing he can do to help her anyway. He disappears into the darkness.

Grant and his mother are talking downstairs. She strains to hear them.

"Come with me to the house," Mrs. Wolcott says.

"But the police—"

"Don't be foolish. They're not coming here. I told them Julian jumped you when you were walking home and stole cash from you. Last you saw him he was running away. Now come up to the house and we'll get that cut cleaned up."

Cassie hears them go out and shut the door. After waiting a few minutes, she leaves as well. One thing is clear. Helen Wolcott is complicit. She knows exactly what Grant did. And she'll clearly do whatever is necessary to protect him.

No wonder she didn't want Cassie dating him in the future. Julian's former girlfriend? A very bad idea. What if she became curious about what really happened?

Chapter Twenty-Seven

OUTSIDE, the rain whips into her. She moves behind a tree on the Wolcott property, considering her options. She knows what Julian is going to do next. But there isn't time for her to follow after him.

She looks out toward the water, realizing she only has one chance to reach him. Thinking about it will only cause fear and hesitation. Instead she sets off across the lawn and when she reaches the dock, she goes to the very end of it, squinting toward the harbor, searching for any sign of him.

The ocean swells are larger than she's ever seen them. Waves crash against the shore on the other side of the channel. Meanwhile the wind-driven rain pushes against her, soaking her hair and clothes, chilling her bones. The howl of the gale makes her want to clap her hands over her ears.

She sees the lights of the vessel before the sound of its engine reaches her. A desperate Julian fleeing in the lobsterboat. He knows the evidence against him is overwhelming and has no clue how he'll prove his innocence. He probably hopes to gain time by running away. Time to figure out his defense. Time for proof to emerge that Grant is the killer. It isn't a real plan. Julian isn't thinking straight at this point.

Grant has done too effective a job of framing him. The knife from the Reis kitchen. The note that Teresa wrote. There was no name at the top, but anyone would assume it was meant for Julian. The necklace she was probably wearing when she was killed—*Adoro-te*. Again, it could equally have come from Julian or his father. But Julian is the one who went to the cove. The police know that, of course, thanks to his girlfriend back from college, who has told them that the boy she loves, without a doubt, was there at the time of the killing. If she were on the jury, she'd convict him too.

He's taken the boat because officers have surrounded his house. Even if he could reach his truck, he would not get far in it with police watching the highways, searching for him. Escaping in the boat was the natural second choice for him.

As he passes near the Wolcott dock, she calls out to him. He doesn't turn, probably didn't hear her over the onslaught of rain and wind. She shouts again. "Julian! Over here!"

He looks now and slows the engine. He's close enough she can see his anxious expression. "Go home, Cass!" He waves her away and continues on.

"Take me with you!" she cries.

He stays the course. She can't let him go without her. An insane idea comes to her, similar to when she slashed her wrist. If she hesitates, he'll be too far away, and she'll never get him back. So she steps off the dock into the roiling sea.

Oh my god, it's so cold, so cold. When she rises for air, she's gasping. This might be it; she might die here and now, and never return to the future. They'll find her prone body with her mind erased.

But then Julian looks back and does a double-take. He

must've seen she's no longer on the dock. "Cass!" he calls out. He cuts the engine and scans the water, looking for her.

"Here, Julian!" She swims toward the boat, but the swells threaten to overwhelm her.

"Fuck." Julian tosses out a lifesaver. He draws her in, lifts her into the boat. "You're crazy," he says, holding her close.

"Take me with you."

He stares at her, gauging her resolve. The waves rock them dangerously. "I have to get the helm." He takes the wheel and directs them out toward open ocean. She stands beside him, shivering and clutching his arm for balance.

"You can find something warm in the hold. And a life-jacket," he says.

She stumbles down the steps to get below deck. Removing her soaked top, she pulls on a man's sweatshirt she finds hanging on a hook. She grabs two lifejackets, puts one on, and brings the other to Julian. She clings to his side while he steers, and they shout over the blasting wind.

"Guess I should've checked the forecast," he says.

"You ever been out in weather this bad?"

He surveys the mounting swells, his face grim. She takes that as a *no*.

Julian nods toward shore. "I can let you off at the point."

"Only if you come with me."

He throws her a look and holds his course. She wraps her hand around his arm. Heavy rain pelts the front windshield. The wipers slap the glass furiously. The waves loom ever larger. But when she looks at Julian, she's shocked to see an excited glow in his face. Amazingly, the challenge of navi-gating through this storm from hell has invigorated him. Her, on the other hand… she's struggling to swallow her panic.

Glimpsing the lighthouse through the darkness ahead of them, she says, "What's next on our love-making tour?"

His lips curl into a smile. "The train, after we ditch the boat in Boston."

"Where will the train take us?"

"Maine. Then we'll cross over into Canada."

"We've never done it in Canada."

"There are lots of lighthouses."

"Something different," she says.

"King's Landing, then. New Brunswick."

"Why there?"

"King's Landing? You know."

She laughs because that's the meaning of *Reis*. King. "It's calling your name."

The boat tips port side and she loses her grip. He reaches out to grasp her arm and pulls her back to him.

"You were crazy to come out here in weather like this," she says.

"I'll take it a million times over being locked up in a cell."

"What about Brumewich? How can you leave your home behind?"

Julian taps on his heart. "It's in here. It's always gonna be here. Same as you."

Farer's Light looms ahead. Waves crash with terrible force against its walls. Julian, momentarily distracted, returns his attention to the helm. He fights to keep the boat steady.

"Forgive me," she says.

"Nothing to forgive. Grant caused this. Not you, or me, or my father. Just Grant."

"You're right. He did this. He has to pay. I swear to god, I'll make him pay."

Julian wraps his arm around her waist, pulling her so tight it hurts. "I believe you, Cass."

They're both unprepared when the wave rises up and washes over them. The force of the water tears Cassie from his grasp, dragging her with it off the boat, under the sea. She tumbles downward.

All is lost. She doesn't even want to help herself. She doesn't think she can live with knowing he was true to her, always. She should've known him better. She should've trusted him.

But her instincts do what her mind won't. Her lungs are in agony. *Must get air.* She raises her arms and pulls hard toward the surface. Not even sure if she's headed the right way.

She feels it then. Julian's hand reaching out to her. She grasps it and he holds her tight. Draws her to the surface. She splutters and chokes, struggling for breath.

They both turn at a flicker of light. Another vessel approaches in the distance. Julian pulls her onto the lifesaver he must've taken from the boat. "Hold on!"

But as she clings to it, a swell surges over him. When it passes, he's gone.

She turns to the boat, almost upon them now. It's the Coast Guard ship sent out to find Julian. "Help! He's drowning!" she shouts.

Divers are ready. The boat slows and they jump in. One locks her in a lifesaver's hold. The other dives under the water. A moment later he surfaces with Julian. Her lover's eyes seek hers and grow calm. It's the last thing she sees before her mind drifts away.

Chapter Twenty-Eight

IT'S OVER. Cassie has learned all she can. Now she needs to regenerate. It's Friday, and she's already begged off work for today. She has till Monday to decide if she wants to return to that job or not.

She's catching up on everything she's neglected, trying to regain some sense of normalcy. Do the laundry. Clean the toilets. Dust and vacuum the house. Pay the bills and balance the checkbook. Shave. Clip her nails. Take a very long shower. Change into fresh clothing. And play with Gio— her sweet, wonderful, adorable companion who still tolerates her unconditionally despite her unintentional neglect of him.

In the evening she gets into bed early, though she's afraid she might time jump in spite of herself. Fortunately, this doesn't happen. Somehow her body understands she's finished what she needed to do. When she wakes in the morning, she feels better rested than she has since the whole surreal experience began.

Her promise to Julian remains foremost in her mind. She's never been more serious than when she swore to make

Grant pay. It won't be easy. He killed a woman and got away with it. Though she's now a witness to that act, she's well aware no court of law will accept testimony provided by a self-proclaimed time-traveler. Moreover, she has no physical evidence, unless she counts her knowledge of the ring he bought for Teresa. But it's not proof of murder.

The phone rings after she's eaten breakfast and she feels sure it must be Grant. The thought makes her insides clamp up, but she makes herself answer. She can't avoid him forever, and she'd rather get it over with sooner rather than later.

"Hello?" She tries to sound relaxed, not like someone who's afraid a cold-blooded killer is calling.

"Cassie, hi," Grant says. "How are you feeling?"

"Much better." This at least is true.

"Are you up to having dinner with me this evening?"

Sorry, Jack the Ripper has me tonight. She doesn't say this, though she'd like to. She's hesitating, wondering if a delay of several more days will help her or not.

But then the word, "Sure," slips out before she can stop it.

"Pick you up at seven?"

"That works."

After they hang up, she doesn't move for several minutes while terror builds inside her. What has she done?

Chapter Twenty-Nine

CASSIE IS in the barn finishing a drawing in pastels when she hears his car drive over the gravel and his door come open and shut. His footsteps create a feeling like ants running up and down her spine. But she has Julian's *Rêverie* playing in the background, and it gives her a measure of courage.

"Grant? I'm in the barn," she calls out to him.

"Hey there," he says, striding into her studio. To anyone else, he probably looks the same as always, but to her, he's taken on a sinister quality. His eyes, a lackluster blue, appear void of feeling. His hands—which she instantly pictures around her neck—are suffused with menace.

She forces herself not to shrink back as he approaches with swift steps, hugs her, and tries to kiss her. She turns her face just in time for his lips to brush her cheek instead.

He draws back to look at her. "Everything okay?"

"Sure." She reaches past him to turn off the music.

"Ready to go?" he says. He may be wondering why she hasn't put any effort into her appearance this evening. She's wearing a T-shirt, jeans, and sandals.

"Wouldn't you like to see my drawing? You were very anxious to look at my sketchpad last time you were here."

He's puzzled by her tone. "Yeah, okay." He shows a distinct lack of enthusiasm, for which she can't blame him. She's sure he doesn't want to see more pictures of Julian.

She leads him to her easel and steps out of the way to give him the full view. It's a sketch of Grant, actually. Standing outside Julian's house. He holds a large kitchen knife that he's about to slip into his backpack. She's witnessed this scene quite recently and was able to hold it in her memory long enough to capture it fairly well. The perspective is hers, from the second-floor window where she looked out and saw him.

"What the…?" he says.

"Do you like it?"

"What the hell is this supposed to be?"

"Can't you tell? I think it's pretty clear. That's Julian's house, in case you're unsure."

"Do you think this is funny?" he says.

"Not funny. Just accurate."

"This never happened."

"Well then, you have nothing to worry about," she says.

"Are you trying to blackmail me?"

"How could I, if it never happened?"

She watches his brain churning. *How do I find out how she knows this without admitting it happened?*

"The picture is a lie. I've never been outside Julian's with a knife. So why draw it?" he says.

She needs to take this further now. "I felt it was time. We've gotten to know each other pretty well over the past few weeks. At least, I feel as if I know you. I've been more distant, but I'd like to change that. You might be surprised to learn we're very much alike."

She's catching his interest now. "I was there the night she was murdered. At Julian's. I was watching you."

Is she imagining it, or does the blood drain from his face? "I was in his bedroom when I heard you come into the house," she continues. "I hid in his closet. I watched you read the note and take it away."

He can't doubt that she's telling the truth at this point. Because he can't imagine any other way she could know exactly what he did in Julian's room.

"I went to the window when you were leaving and saw you put the knife in your backpack," she says. "The knife you used to frame him. Oh, and I also saw you throw out the note in their garbage can."

He struggles to find his voice. "You're making this shit up. I don't understand why. Especially after all this time."

"I told you. We're alike. Well, I don't imagine I could actually have killed her, especially not with a knife. I really don't like looking at blood. I suppose I could poison someone if I had to. But that's neither here nor there. I was glad you killed her. And glad you made Julian take the fall for it. I hated them both for what they did to me." This part of her speech is much harder to get through, but she manages it.

"Have you told anyone about this fantasy of yours?"

"I'm not sure I should answer that question. Are you threatening me?" she says.

"Of course not. But if you mean what you say, and you're really on my side, you wouldn't be going around telling people that I killed someone."

"Probably not," she agrees.

"And what about the police? Did you tell this bullshit story to them?"

"That wouldn't be very smart of me, would it? I'd look really bad for not having said anything seven years ago. I'm pretty sure they could arrest me for withholding evidence. They might even figure I was your accomplice."

This next part is the hardest. She leans into Grant and gives him a long, slow, luxurious kiss. At the end she says, "I've kept your secret all these years. I'm not about to give it away now."

Then, as if this has been the most casual conversation in the world, she adds, "Shall we go now?"

Chapter Thirty

NEEDLESS TO SAY, they don't go. It would've been the most uncomfortable meal since Salome served up John the Baptist's head. Grant says, "Are you fucking kidding me? Dinner's off."

"I get it," she says. "Take your time thinking it over. In the end, I hope you'll understand you can be honest with me. Like I've been with you."

She's never seen anyone gun their car out of her driveway so fast. Buckets of gravel shoot out behind his tires.

Once he's left, she returns to the house and locks up carefully. Having predicted Grant would back out of their dinner date, she ate early and washed it down with a cup of coffee. Now she pours herself a second cup and brings it with her into the family room. It's still early so she switches on the TV to distract herself. She keeps changing the channel because there isn't anything entertaining enough to pry her thoughts from the contemplation of Grant's next steps.

At least Gio comes to her lap and soothes her with his gentle purrs. When the sun finally sets, however, she puts him outside and latches his cat door shut to keep him out of the house until morning. He'll be fine. The weather is warm, and he knows how to take care of himself. She's only trying to protect him from possible harm. If anything happens.

She gathers a few items she'd like to keep with her tonight and turns out all the downstairs lights before heading upstairs. When she's finished using the bathroom, she gets into her mother's bed without changing into pajamas and turns out the lamp beside her. The house is completely dark now. The coffee has made her sleepless, leaving her with little to do aside from staring up at the ceiling, remembering her vow to Julian.

Eventually, she doesn't know when, she drifts to sleep, until the splintering of glass downstairs wakes her. Her eyes snap open and shift to the clock, which shows 2:13 a.m. She sits up and quietly lifts the phone receiver. She's about to place the call when she realizes there's no dial tone. Her hands tremble. *Fuck.* She hadn't meant to fall asleep. She'd hoped to hear him and use the phone before he had a chance to cut the line. He's been admirably stealthy. No doubt she heard nothing because he came on his bike. A car is much more noticeable and likely to be witnessed. Cassie knows something about that.

It's going to be much harder now.

Slipping out of the bed, she takes the two long pillows she brought up from the family room and places them under the blanket. With a little adjustment, they resemble the shape of a person close enough.

Sounds of falling glass come from the back of the house. He must be reaching in and opening the sliding door. Soon he'll be here.

She reaches under the bed for her father's bat that she placed there earlier. Though she's not religious, she blows a kiss up toward the sky. Knowing how many times his hands gripped this wood gives her courage.

The stairs creak once. Twice. Time is running out. She crouches on the other side of the dresser. He'll need to enter the room fully so she can swing at him. She's practiced the move, though she's no baseball player—a fact that sorely disappointed her father.

She hears the squeak of a door being pushed open. He's checking her bedroom first. Next will come the study and bathroom before he reaches here. She clenches the bat and gets ready. All at once, the room feels sweltering. Sweat oozes out of her pores.

A footstep sounds just outside the door. He pauses to take stock, she thinks. A few seconds later, he moves forward into the room, approaching the bed. Glimpsing him from her hiding place, she sees a loop of rope in his hand. How kind of him not to use a knife. He must've remembered she doesn't like the sight of blood.

He's about to lift off the blanket and discover the pillows. She has to act. Vaulting up, she takes a great swing with the bat, aiming at his head. But two things happen. One, her sweaty grip slips and fails to deliver as fast and hard a blow as needed. Two, he's so much quicker than she could've imagined. Raising his hand, he blocks the impact. She might've hurt his wrist, no more than that.

Knowing she won't get another chance, she drops the bat and leaps past him while he's still staggering. She races toward the stairs as his steps start thumping behind her. "Bitch!" he calls out.

She flies down to the first floor and turns toward the front door, but he's faster, gaining on her. He leaps and tackles her. Flashback to the beach as she crashes to the floor, but this time she fights harder, squirming and managing to turn so she's on her back facing him.

He sits on her, pinning her, pressing her wrists against the hard floor. She struggles to escape, kicking at him, raising her head to try to bite his arm. But then he lifts her right hand and slams it with incredible force against the wood. She screams in agony. The pain is excruciating. She's sure he's broken something.

"If you don't stop moving, I'll do that again," he says.

She grows still, waiting to see what's coming next. Tears leak down the side of her cheeks.

"It won't help you to kill me," she says. "I've told someone else all about you. If I die, she'll know it was you."

"I don't believe you. Who would you tell? You're like a hermit here. You don't have any friends."

"I sent a letter to my mother. She'll go to the police if you do anything to me."

"Your mother," he says. "I don't believe you. No way would you tell her you knew I was guilty and did nothing. You watched me take the murder weapon and didn't even try to stop me. You'd die before admitting that to her."

"Let me go!"

"Sorry. I can't allow you to create trouble for me." He moves his legs onto her upper arms to free up his hands briefly. With swift movements, he takes the rope from his jacket pocket, yanks her hair to lift her head, and slips the rope around her neck. Her head bangs when he drops it, but the pain is nothing compared to the sensation of the rope being tightened around her wind pipe.

Oh god, oh god. She thrashes her body, trying to hide her real purpose. Struggling to force her throbbing hand into her pocket. She would be screaming if she had air. She barely manages to grasp the jackknife and pull it out. But opening it with one broken hand… it isn't working… though she practiced for hours earlier.

As her lungs burn and she starts to lose her sight, the knife springs open. She thrusts it into his ass, the only part of him she can reach. He cries out and loses his grip on the rope. She sucks in air and jabs him with the knife again, this time his belly. He tumbles sideways, staring in disbelief at the blood spewing out.

She wastes no time shoving past him, scrambling to her feet, darting to the door. *Why didn't I leave it open?* It all takes time, snapping the bolt, turning the knob, pulling the door open. Already Grant is forcing himself up. A glance back shows her he's in an absolute rage.

The door swings wide and she vaults to the driveway, heading toward the street, aiming for her neighbor's house across it. She wants to scream but barely a whisper comes out from her scratched and damaged throat.

Grant's steps crunch the gravel in back of her. He grabs her shirt from behind; it tears as she keeps running. He reaches for her arm, his clammy fingers grip her, when lights appear in the distance.

They're headlights from a car turning onto her street. Grant's hands slip away from her. She keeps running, waving her arms, as the car races toward them. The police. They swerve into her driveway, brake hard. The doors fly open. Two men leap out, one who she recognizes as Officer Brooks, the nice man who helped her betray Julian.

They go after Grant, who's now dashing between the house and the barn, dripping blood in his wake. She follows behind, wondering what he's doing, because there's nothing back there but water.

Before they can reach him, he splashes into the harbor and dives beneath the surface. She guesses police aren't prepared for swimming pursuits—with all their heavy equipment they'd sink like boulders. The two officers stop at the edge and call out to Grant, ordering him to stop and come back. When he doesn't, one lights the water with the spray of his flashlight, while the other gets out his gun and shoots. She can't tell if a bullet strikes him or not, but it isn't long before the surface is still as glass and there's no further sight of him.

It doesn't surprise her Grant chose the water. He was of Brumewich after all. The sea doesn't distinguish between wicked and virtuous when it calls its creatures home.

Chapter Thirty-One

THREE DAYS LATER, the sea spits out what's left of Grant Wolcott at Thorne Cove. It didn't want him after all, and was clever enough to send him back to the scene of his unforgivable crime.

After two weeks have passed, Cassie is ready to move on. With her one hand in a splint, she gathers up the mementos of Julian she's kept all these years and puts the sealed box in storage. Briefly she considers throwing it out, but decides baby steps are sufficient for now.

Quitting her job has freed up her time. She's sure Maggie was happy to see her go, though her boss kindly pretended her departure would be a big loss to them. Maggie even offered to give her an excellent recommendation, despite that she's terrible at sales. She can't be bothered to try to convince anyone to buy something they're not already sure they'll love.

As she's brushing off dust and spiderwebs that came of her trip to the attic, the doorbell rings. Happily, the sound no longer makes her want to flee out the rear exit.

It's Officer Brooks. This will be the first time they've

spoken since the night he and Officer Fanshawe rescued her. In the light of day, she sees he's changed in the years since Teresa's murder. The worry lines on his forehead and flecks of darkness in his eyes show the toll his work exacts.

She ushers him into the kitchen and offers him coffee, which he accepts. They sit across from each other at the table, him with his notepad and pencil.

"Do you have any questions for me before we get started?" he says.

"No one has told me who called you to my house." In all the madness of that night, she didn't think to ask.

"It was Helen Wolcott."

His answer astonishes her. "Mrs. Wolcott?"

"She told us she was concerned when Grant came home that evening in a fury. He wouldn't tell her what it was about, but she knew he'd been planning to take you to dinner."

"I'm still baffled. How did this lead to her calling the police at two-thirty in the morning?"

He swallows a sip of coffee. "Mrs. Wolcott had hired a man to watch her son."

"Seriously?"

"She wanted someone to keep an eye on him. The problem was, the guy fell asleep on the job. Otherwise we would've been here right away. Because when he finally woke up, he saw Grant's bike was gone, reported to Mrs. Wolcott, and she called us."

"Why was she having him watched?" She's starting to think she must've completely misunderstood the woman.

Officer Brooks lowers his cup. "She suspected he was responsible for Teresa's murder. And since then, she's apparently been tortured by the fear he might kill again. It worried her deeply when he started dating you. Another girl who'd had a relationship with Julian Reis, right?"

With nothing to gain by revealing Armando, not Julian, had dated Teresa, she remains silent.

"Mrs. Wolcott was concerned about his motives," he says. "Did he think you might know something? Could you be a threat to him?"

She wonders if it's much simpler than Mrs. Wolcott imagined. In Grant's eyes, Julian stole the love of his life. Grant's narcissism required he do the same in return.

"I'll be honest," he says. "Mrs. Wolcott often comes across as haughty. But she's clearly a woman of principle. My impression is she couldn't live with herself if her son killed again on her watch."

"I understand. I'm indebted to her. She saved my life." Cassie would not go so far as to call her a woman of principle. She'd been willing to lie for her murdering son. But at least she took action to prevent it from happening again. Her unsuccessful attempt to drive Cassie away from Grant had not been motivated by snobbery after all.

Officer Brooks raises his pencil. "A few things puzzle me."

"Go on."

"When did you begin to suspect Grant killed Teresa?"

When a meteorite landed and granted me the gift of travel through time. No, she doesn't say this. Instead, she weaves a tale that begins with Grant's uncomfortable reactions to her sketches of Julian and an accidental visit to Teresa's grave.

"I decided to test Grant," she lies. "I let on I had a friend who thought he and Teresa had a relationship. I asked if it was true and he angrily denied it. But the most interesting part was how hard he tried to get the name of my 'friend.'

"On another occasion, I led him into a discussion of jewelry. He told me his favorite place to buy gifts is Dorn Jewelers in Boston. So just to test him, I said in a teasing way,

I guess one way to find out if you ever dated Teresa would be to ask Dorn to check their receipts."

"Interesting," Officer Brooks says. "We opened a safe in his office and found an engagement ring that came from there. Grant's and Teresa's initials engraved inside."

She nods her head. "It doesn't surprise me." *Since I've seen that ring before*, she doesn't say.

"Grant went ballistic over the jewelry thing," she goes on. "I managed to patch it up, sort of. Meanwhile, I was thinking if he killed her, he must've framed Julian somehow. Grant could easily have taken the knife from his house. You know it was always unlocked, don't you?"

She gets up, removes a drawing from where she left it in a drawer, and shows it to the officer. It isn't the original one she drew, which she destroyed. This one shows Grant leaving the house holding a knife, without details like the backpack. She doesn't want Officer Brooks thinking she must've been there and seen it with her own eyes.

"When I showed this to Grant, I knew from the look on his face that I'd guessed right. This happened on the evening before he attacked me," she says.

"You shouldn't have provoked him," he says. "You almost got yourself killed."

"It was the only way to force a confession out of him."

"He confessed?"

"Oh yes," she says. "He told me everything." It was true he confessed, but not that he revealed everything. She added that to protect herself if she ever slips up and reveals she knows more about the murder than she possible could.

"What good would the confession be if you were dead? Right? You took a terrible risk."

"I did try to defend myself, but as you know, that didn't go terribly well. Still, I also sent a letter to my mother, telling her what I'm telling you now. She would've brought it to you if I was killed." What she told Grant was another half-truth. She'd written to her mother, but there was nothing in the letter about hiding in Julian's house and watching Grant steal the knife.

"Why go so far to prove Grant guilty?" he says, though she thinks at this point he knows the answer.

"For Julian, of course. I did it for him."

Chapter Thirty-Two

CASSIE'S HEALTH IS RESTORED. She's eating normally again and the headaches and exhaustion have disappeared. She still isn't sure whether these were side effects of the time travel, or the result of her mania to discover the truth and reveal it to the world. In the end, it doesn't matter.

In real life, Julian didn't survive his attempt to escape in the boat. In the past—the real past—she never went to Grant's house, never knew Grant was involved in any way. She never beckoned to Julian from the Wolcott dock, never jumped in the water to make him stop for her. Instead, she waited with Armando for his son who never came home.

The overturned boat was found near Farer's Light with no one onboard. All lifejackets were accounted for in its hold, meaning Julian hadn't been wearing one. It was she, in the altered past, who made him put it on. A man who'd spent his life on boats ought to have known better. Maybe the rush to get away, and the strain of navigating through an unrelenting storm, kept him from taking the most basic steps to ensure his safety. Or maybe it was a choice.

Unlike with Grant, the sea swallowed Julian and kept him as its own.

Armando moved to New Bedford several months later. He said his lobstering days were over, though she's not certain what he planned to do instead. At some point, he must've considered telling the police he was the one in a relationship with Teresa. But it wouldn't have cleared Julian's name. After all, it was Julian who met with Teresa at Thorne Cove, and Julian who fled in the boat. These actions gave him all the appearance of guilt, and nothing Armando might've said could change it.

Cassie is moving to Boston in a few weeks. Her mother and Freddie are coming home to stay. "Florida's too hot in the summer," her mother said. "We can visit in winter."

She isn't certain what she'll do in the city, but it will have some relation to art. Maybe she'll find work as an assistant at a museum or gallery. Or she might pursue a degree in education that will allow her to teach. For the first time, the possibilities intrigue her, and the thought of leaving Brumewich no longer frightens her.

Julian had it right all along. You carry the things you love inside you.

She's about to take one last jump, and then she'll be done. Tomorrow she'll paddle out to the middle of Inner Harbor in her canoe and drop the meteorite into the water. She hopes that will keep her from ever trying to use it again.

After settling in bed with Gio beside her, she spins back to the place of her memory. She's just arrived outside Julian's house on Christmas Eve during her winter break from Syracuse. Snow has covered the yard in a thick, inviting blanket, but she resists the urge to wrap herself in it.

The window by the door is adorned with orange lights in the shape of a lobster. It's been a staple of their Christmas decorations for as long as she can remember. She knocks once before letting herself in.

Armando greets her on his way out. "Where are you going on Christmas Eve?" she says.

He carries a large red envelope and a small, wrapped box. She thinks it must be the necklace etched with the words, "Adoro-te," which he's bringing to the woman he loves. She imagines the poem *Para Teresa* written inside the card.

"It's a secret." He winks at her.

When he's gone, she and Julian sit by the fireplace and exchange gifts. He receives a painting she did of his mother from a photograph Armando loaned her. She gets a handknit hat and scarf that might've been purchased from Teresa.

"Play *Rêverie* for me," she says.

When he sits at the piano, she stands behind him with her arms around his shoulders, leaning into him.

As the beloved melody flows through her like the sea, she presses her face against his neck. After the last note is played, she moves beside him on the bench and he draws her into his lap, holding her close.

She whispers her last words to him. "You and me forever, Reis." She taps her hand against her heart.

THE END

Read on for a sample of *Before She Was Taken*
(The Before Series Book Two).

MOONLIGHT SPILLS across the frayed mustard carpet to reach Nicki, splayed on her back atop the rock-hard mattress of her bed. The brightness wakes her as she had intended. At bedtime, Mother had lowered the shades, but Nicki had quietly raised them after she left.

The time is three in the morning. Her hands tingle as she rises and puts on her heavy blue hoodie over her pajamas. She crosses to the chair, trying not to look at the yellowed wallpaper with pictures of little girls in pigtails playing on a slide, on a swing set, in a sandbox, and splashing in a baby pool. However much Nicki grows—she turned sixteen last month—it feels like she's forever trapped inside the moments of childhood depicted on these four walls.

She picks up Cinderella, a large stuffed bear with one eye missing, and reaches under her skirt through the hole she slashed into her long ago. With the stuffing removed, the space serves as a hiding place for any cash she manages to steal, and for the treats she saves for Sadie. Nicki removes half of a Hershey's chocolate bar and pockets it before putting on her sneakers and tiptoeing to the door.

With practiced caution, she turns the knob, slips through the narrow opening, and silently closes the door behind her. She pauses to listen to Uncle's gruntlike snores from the room next to hers. It gives her some courage to confirm he's asleep. Unfortunately, she can't be certain about Mother, in the bedroom across the hall, who never makes a sound that can be heard outside her room.

Nicki proceeds to the stairs and descends them with delicate steps, careful to avoid the parts that creak the loudest. She's almost at the bottom and ready to congratulate herself, when the wood groans under her foot. Freezing in place, she listens for sounds of stirring.

After a minute passes without anyone coming, she decides it's safe to continue. Thankfully, the hall and kitchen have linoleum floors that allow her to cross quietly. The drawer, on the other hand, sticks to its frame and makes a horrible noise if she's not careful. She must open it for the flashlight, though, and she manages well enough. She'll worry about closing it later.

She takes a water bottle from the box by the counter before snatching the key to the shed from behind one of the shelves. Some time ago, she discovered where Uncle kept it by spying on him from inside the pantry.

Her last hurdle is the back door, so tight in its frame it has to be yanked open. It makes some noise and even rattles the house a bit, but it's too late to turn back now. She escapes outside and down the steps, where she pauses for a gulp of the brisk air scented with pine. A shiver skips down her spine at the sight of the moonlit trees, lurking around the edge of the property like rows of tall, spindly jailers.

She dashes across the carpet of pine needles to get to the

shed, and lets herself in with the key, closing the door after her. Switching on the flashlight, she's careful not to aim it at the bed since no one likes to be woken with bright light in their eyes.

Four-year-old Sadie is curled under the blanket looking up at her. Her hair is matted and there's a dark smudge on her left cheek. She sucks on the tip of her thumb, with a filthy, threadbare rabbit missing most of its stuffing clutched under her arm.

Nicki sits on the mattress beside her and touches her hair. "Hey there," she whispers.

Sadie lowers her thumb. "Hey."

"I brought you a treat." Nicki takes out the chocolate bar.

Sadie sits up and leans against the wall. "Thank you."

"Should we have a tea party?"

Sadie nods.

Nicki arranges the rabbit and a stuffed dog with a monocle on either side of them. Recovering four plastic teacups piled in the corner, she sets them in front of everyone and pours a bit of water into the cups. "Sugar?"

"Yes, two please," Sadie says.

Nicki drops imaginary sugar cubes into her cup and turns to the rabbit. "Becca?"

"One half, please." Nicki provides the high-pitched voice of Becca the rabbit.

Pretending to struggle to break the cube in half, Nicki speaks in an aside to Sadie. "She only wants to make things difficult."

"I heard that," the rabbit voice replies.

"Mr. Fluffernutter doesn't need any. He doesn't like sweets," Sadie says regarding the dog.

"They, hem, interfere with my digestion." Nicki lends Mr. Fluffernutter a deep growly tone.

Sadie places a piece of her chocolate in front of Becca.

"I'd like half of that," the rabbit says.

"No!" Sadie says, laughing.

"Tomorrow let's take Becca to the salon and get her fur done," Nicki says.

"I went there yesterday!" Sadie does the rabbit voice. "Can't you tell?"

"Oh my, and a beautiful job they did too." Nicki winks at Sadie.

"Mr. Fluffernutter should get a pedicure," Sadie says.

"Hem, only if I may get the purple glitter polish," is Mr. Fluffernutter's response.

Sadie sips from her cup. "I want to see my mommy."

Nicki glances back toward the house. "Mother's sleeping now."

"Not her." Sadie makes a face. "My real mommy."

"She's your real mommy now. And he's your uncle."

Sadie shakes her head hard. Her face crumples and tears start to flow.

"Come here." Nicki moves everything out of the way and sits beside her holding the girl's hand in her lap. "You have to be patient. Things that are important take time."

"I miss her," Sadie whispers.

"I know. I'll take care of you. You have to trust me." But even as the words emerge from her lips, she hears the heavy shoes pounding down the back steps of the house and rushing toward them.

End of preview.

Please visit margiebenedict.com for purchase options.

Acknowledgments

Much love and gratitude to my cherished first readers: Harriet Benedict, Sheri Davenport, Tanner Kaptanoglu, Kay Liscomb, Susan Rendina, and Karla Sheridan. Any mistakes that remain are purely my own.

To the many indie authors who belong to the Facebook group, *Wide for the Win*: thank you for sharing your wisdom and experience. May mountains of writing and publishing success—however you define it—come to you all.

About the Author

Margie Benedict writes emotionally resonant, genre-defying fiction rooted in the power of second chances. From coastal suspense to time-twisted mysteries and sweeping speculative worlds, her stories follow characters who rise, reclaim their agency, and rewrite their destinies.

Formerly publishing as Marjory Kaptanoglu, Margie is an award-winning author praised by Kirkus, Publishers Weekly, and the BookLife Prize. Her work blends gripping tension with deep emotional stakes, drawing comparisons to *The Time Traveler's Wife*, *Outlander*, and the twist-driven novels of Lisa Jewell.

Before turning to fiction full-time, she developed pioneering software at Apple Computer and wrote screenplays that were recognized by the Nicholl Fellowships and produced for film.

Margie is now building a brand readers can trust for gripping, transformative storytelling—books that don't just entertain but empower. From middle grade fantasy to adult thrillers, sci-fi, and women's fiction, she invites readers of all ages to ask: *What would you do with a second chance?*

www.ingramcontent.com/pod-product-compliance
Lightning Source LLC
Chambersburg PA
CBHW030855200726
48289CB00003B/761